A DINO RIFT SEQUEL

SAURA CORPS:
SALVATION

A DINO RIFT SEQUEL

SAURA CORPS:
SALVATION

DEREK BORNE

SAURACORPS: SALVATION

Edited by R.A. Milhoan Book Services
Cover Design and Interior Formatting by We Got You Covered Book Design
WWW.WEGOTYOUCOVEREDBOOKDESIGN.COM
Photograph of Derek Borne by Tara Jeles – So Jeles Photography
Dinosaur Sketches by Devon Kahles @devonkahles_art

Published by Virtuoso Press

TO MOM,

*Thank you for being the inspiration for
the "Baskin Robbins" line in Dino-Rift.
And for being my mom, of course.*

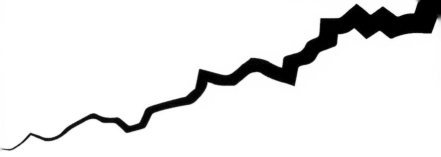

ONE

"**SOMEONE BETTER** receive this package before they *rip a damn hole* in the side of my transport." The frustrated truck driver had spoken into the radio com as he pulled into the loading area. It was the middle of the night, and his cargo wasn't the only cranky creature on board. "The last five minutes have been—"

THWAM! SMASH!

"Jeez!" He flinched as the cargo trailer behind him rocked side to side.

A response came through. *"We're locking onto you now."*

From both sides of the cargo bay, mechanical arms unfolded and attached to the trailer with heavy-duty suction cups.

The driver scratched at his balding head before opening his cab door to take a better look. "This some kind of new NASA type stuff?"

A chuckle came from the person on the other end.

"Something like that."

The last clasp had suctioned into position.

RAWR-RAWR-RAAAAWR!

"My God...." Half-stumbling back into his seat, the man squeezed the radio com tighter. "I've never had a delivery this agitated before. What the heck's in there?"

"All this time, you've been paid enough to not *ask those questions, Gary."*

About to fire back a remark, the driver took a moment to wipe the glistening sweat from his brow. Gary's bank account had never dropped below fifty-thousand for a year and a half. His family always ate to satisfaction.

All thanks to ignorance.

More feral growls preceded a creaking sway from the back end.

It all pressed on his inquisitiveness like a floored gas pedal. Regaining his dignity, he spoke into the com. "Starting to wonder if it's still worth it." Once he'd tossed the piece of radio equipment onto the seat, he climbed out of the cab and swung the door shut with a clang.

He kept his gaze on the receiving overhead door while instinctively withdrawing his cellphone from a jacket pocket.

Mechanical noises indicated the acceptance of the 'package'.

GRRRR-RAAAAWR!

Within the facility, shouts and yells were muffled by the walls.

Gary let curses fly under his breath. "Nope. No more."

Facial recognition brought up the apps on his phone.

He clicked on the call app and began dialing three simple numbers.

Two rings later, a receptionist picked up.

"Nine-one-one, what's your emergency?"

Now that the call had connected, Gary looked back at his transport truck. The vehicle which had carried countless cargo, which had also made his life a lot simpler.

"Hello? Is there an emergency?"

"Y-yes." Gary drew out a breath as his other hand rubbed more sweat off of his forehead. "I'd like to report a disturbance."

"What kind of disturbance?" The woman on the other end added, "Can you describe what's happening?"

He let out an exasperated laugh. "Um, honestly I... I don't even—"

THOK!

The phone dropped to the ground.

Gary's legs gave out.

His right cheek scraped into the asphalt.

"Hello?" The responder took the silence as a negative cue. "Sir? Are you—"

"Sorry to inconvenience you." Someone else wearing a balaclava spoke into the phone. "It's all good."

Before the lady on the other end could reply, they ended the call.

A voice entered the masked man's earpiece. *"Is he incapacitated?"*

"He's out." A kick to Gary's limp foot confirmed it. "Where do you want him?"

A couple of seconds went by. *"Bertha hasn't eaten in a while."*

Already taking Gary by the arms, the man snickered. "He's got some extra meat on his bones, too."

"Get the grate open."

As voices carried back and forth, Gary opened one eye to a slit and took in a humid breath. Scents of rich foliage entered his nostrils.

Off to his left, a quartet of people exerted themselves to lift a heavy metal grill.

Someone grabbed him by the shoulders.

"H-h-hey." Gary came to a little more as he got dragged along. "Get your hands o—*aaaaugh!*"

Whump-snap!

His right shin broke on impact with the hard ground. Yelling out in agony, Gary figured his entire upper body would become a massive bruise. "What…in the…*all freaking heck*…have you—"

"That's it, Gary." The masked man shouted down to him. "Bertha likes it when her *food* makes noise."

Throbbing seared up from his broken leg. "Get me out of here *now,* you pieces of…."

Gary's eyes finally adjusted.

Unfamiliar trees and foliage stood off to his left. Dazed yet super alert to the agonizing pain in his leg, he gazed past the plant life and noticed concrete forming walls on all four sides of him. On the right, unrecognizable and dense vegetation decorated a sizeable area with a nearby water source.

He looked up. It had been at least a hundred-foot drop into the manufactured pit. *Did they just.... Am I underground?*

Things finally clicked in his mind. *This is...some kind of cage?*

A pair of trees creaked as something forced them to lean away from each other. Though it seemed to be sizeable, whatever it was barely made a sound as it moved.

Everything hurt as Gary tried to shimmy himself away. He turned his head to look back, then whipped his gaze back to the front.

A quick flicker of wet flesh struck his scuffed cheek.

Garish reptilian eyes the size of footballs stared down at him.

Its thick forked tongue quivered inches away from his face.

Still as could be, Gary squeezed his eyes almost all the way shut. *I can't go like this. Please...not like this.*

The creature's muscular body shuffled past his injured foot.

Gary opened one of his eyes.

Slithering away, the monstrous animal made little noise through the grass.

Up top, those who had a hand in tossing the man down sighed in disapproval and disappointment.

"Again?" The leading man stared through the grate.

"Freddy, dump the chum."

Already waiting with the bucket, one of the assistants aimed and let the contents descend into the oversized terrarium.

Splish-splash-sploosh.

Soaked in the fish refuse, Gary wiped some of it off of his head. "Ugh, what in the—"

Hissss!

The head of the creature had only made it about thirty feet away.

Another flick of its tongue grabbed onto the scent.

Its eyes connected with Gary's.

In less than five seconds, the animal's head had darted back. The creature arched its neck and opened its mouth wide, revealing lethal fangs.

"No, God sakes, *no!*"

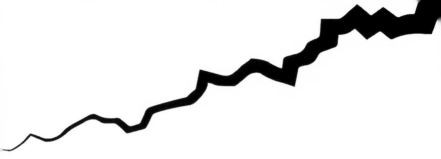

TWO

"THIS IS the place, right?" Less than half a block away, Kamren Eckhardt drove his black pick-up truck down a street in Chicago, Illinois.

Vivienne Lancaster took a better look at the name across the front of a hotel. "It most definitely is."

Once they'd pulled up right outside the entrance, Kam reached for the music volume dial.

"Hey." Viv slapped his hand and gave him a playful smirk. "The song's almost done."

Kam put both hands up in defense. "Whoa, sorry. We've only listened to it *at least fifty times* on this trip."

"True, but *Rule Eighteen.*" Viv didn't even unclip her seatbelt. "No one leaves or turns off the vehicle until the epic song has finished."

Chuckling, Kam cranked the volume up. "That's my girl."

The last run of the chorus of *One Touch* by Jess Glynne

7

and Jax Jones blared throughout the cab of the truck. Stylish pop music with the singer's raspy voice rattled the windows.

Kam and Viv sang their hearts out to each other with the final chorus.

The lyrics moved them to intertwine their hands.

As soon as it finished, Kam pulled her closer to him. "All right, you're too cute, you know that right?"

She kissed him on the lips. "And you were a little off key."

"Excuse me?"

Once they'd taken everything up to their room, Kam and Viv headed back down to the foyer. The two nineteen-year-olds had made it a little over halfway through their road trip from Utah. After their graduation, they'd promised to take their 'compensation money' from SauraCorps to make their first trip to New York City together. Chicago had been on their list of major U.S. cities to visit and tour on the way.

"Lady Lancaster, what have you planned for us on our first day in the 'Windy City'?" Kam strolled out the front door and held it open for her.

Wearing one of his blue hoodies for the early fall weather, Viv chuckled while slipping one of her hands into his. Walking alongside him, she put on her best English accent. "Lord Kamren, we shall first obtain sustenance."

"Ah, but of course." He mimicked the accent and brought her knuckles to his lips for a kiss. "And which fair establishment will you be leading me to after we eat?"

"It's a surprise."

Kam let out an over-the-top gasp. "Is it now?"

"Yep." Looking away from his gaze, as his eyes tended to make her all warm and gooey on the inside, she pressed her lips together tight.

"Vivieeeenne…." He drew out her name in a lower tone.

She made no reply as they made a left turn on the sidewalk.

"I see how it is."

Still saying nothing, she squint-glared at him.

"If I must barrage your face with kisses to get my answers…" Kam stopped mid-step and pulled her back into him. He kept trying to make his gaze connect with her teal eyes. "…then I most certainly will."

She managed to keep his sultry stare at bay as she chuckled. "Dude, not in public, okay?"

"That didn't sound British." He pulled back a step. "It's been a year and a half since we went official, and just now you don't like PDA?"

"I don't want to make all of Chicago uncomfortable with my affection for you," she reasoned, poking him in the side. "Now come on, my stomach's about to growl like a giganotosaurus."

"Hey," he remarked with a smirk. "You pronounced that well."

"I've had some practice."

They approached a crosswalk and had to wait for the lights to turn.

Kam leaned into her side. "Can I at least give your cheek

a peck?"

Viv grinned. "As you wish."

A quick kiss later, Kam spotted a food truck with an eclectic menu decaled on the side. "Let's grab something from that dude."

After crossing, they stepped into the line with a few people left to order at the takeout window.

"As much as this trip will be epic, I'm more excited about moving in and really starting a life together." Viv's face beamed as she spoke. "I'll start my online handmade jewelry shop, you'll be publishing your books."

"It'll feel even more real when I get those apartment keys in my hands," Kam added, equally eager and nervous for the next steps they were about to take on their journey to adulthood. *And when I get something shiny with diamonds on your hand—*

"Hey there." The food truck owner poked his head out. "What can I get ya?"

It didn't take long for Viv to choose. "Your schnitzel on a pretzel bun sounds amazing. And a water, please."

Kam smirked as he nudged her. "Watch this."

She squinted at him. "What are you—"

"Any chance you guys have a dragonfly on a bun?" He inquired while holding back a silly grin. "And give me all the fixin's."

The food truck owner almost responded, but left his mouth slightly open.

Viv gave her boyfriend a stare as if to say *'Shut up!'*

Puzzled, the man finally responded. "Sorry, did you just

say *dragonfly?*"

Another cook within the truck called over, "Dragonfly? What's he goin' on about?"

"You know." Kam's mouth twitched, keeping a laugh at bay. "Like a prehistoric one. They're superb when roasted over a fire and—"

"Are you okay, young man?" the owner countered with a weirded-out chuckle.

Viv jabbed Kam in the arm with her elbow. "Cut it out."

"Okay, okay." Taking it only that far, Kam glanced at the menu once more. "Sausage on a bun, my good man."

Shaking his head, the owner retreated into the truck. "If you say so."

Meanwhile, Viv had been looking around to see if anyone else had heard the odd conversation going on. "How about you *don't* talk about our escapades in the dinosaur times?"

"Let me answer that with a question." He pulled his wallet out to prepare for when food would be handed out to them. "Who's actually going to believe that we got tossed through a time rift and trekked through prehistoric times?"

Rubbing her tense arms, she raised an eyebrow. "The rift stuff did seem to fade out of the news pretty quickly."

"As per media usual." After curling some of her blonde hair with pink streaks over her left ear, he placed his hands on her shoulders. "Doesn't stop me from wondering what dragonfly would taste like with some sauerkraut and mustard."

"Blegh." Viv overemphasized a barfing noise. "I'd rather eat A.B.C. gum."

Their order came out less than two minutes later. Kam and Viv carried on with their lunch in their hands. The warm summery air coupled with the gourmet street meat gave them plenty to enjoy. Heading north, they caught sight of the entrance to Chicago's main zoo, which sat close to the shore of Lake Michigan.

"Is this our next destination?" Kam chewed on one of his last bites.

Viv tossed her water bottle into a nearby recycle can. "Figured it had been forever since we'd been to a zoo."

"We just graduated from one, like, about a year ago—"

"Just buy us tickets already!"

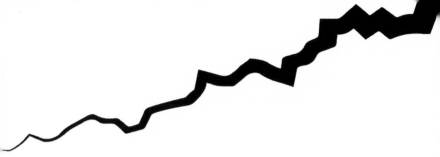

THREE

OVER AT the northeast end of the zoo, one of the veterinarians browsed over paperwork at her desk. Other than treating a camel for ringworm and resetting a penguin's broken wing, it had been a relatively slow past couple of days.

Dr. Kol's open laptop notified her of an incoming e-mail.

Glancing over to the small window in her office door, she got up for a moment to engage the lock, close the blinds, and returned to the desk.

Accessing the e-mail inbox required a password.

Buzzzz. Buzzzz.

Her fingers barely touched the keyboard when her cellphone came to life.

Phone to her ear, she answered, "Did you bring me some lunch, Drew?"

"I've got your falafel bowl right here."

She grinned, excited to once again have a lunch date.

"You remembered the hummus and pickled turnips, right?"

He chuckled. "Sure did, Izzy."

"You know me so—"

"But you're going to have to come *out here.*"

The request seemed vague and odd. Normally, their time together would be within the veterinary facility.

She gazed out the window into the parking lot and spotted his outfitted pick-up truck. "Now why would I—"

"Trust me." His tone swelled with mysterious excitement. "You're going to want to see this thing."

Less than a minute later, Dr. Isabella Kol exited the building and found her new beau and the resident animal wrangler Drew waiting for her in the parking lot's middle lane.

He greeted her with a peck on the cheek, then pointed to a tarped cube-like structure sitting in the back of his truck. "You're not going to believe what I got my hands on last night."

Isabella headed over to the vehicle almost as fast as him. "Are we taking this package *downstairs* for holding?"

Drew opened the tailgate and hopped up into the black bedliner. "Can we get access to it today?" One of the bungee cords keeping the tarp down sprang away as he began unveiling. "I'm sure the others would love to see it, too."

Isabella spied pieces of vertical rebar as more of the green tarp lifted away. "I'll make a call and have the building cleared for a bit."

"Perfect." With one final toss, Drew revealed the whole front of the cage and smiled back at the vet. "Recognize what it is?"

Isabella's eyes scoured the entirety of the large metal crate. "Um…is this a prank?"

"What?" He gave her a confused stare. "No, it's a…." Once he peered in as well, Drew's eyes opened wide. *"Seriously?"*

Alarm rose within Isabella. "Is it dangerous?"

Drew ripped the rest of the tarp off as he tried to determine how the creature had escaped. "It's not supposed to be, but… Jeez, how the heck did it…." Coming around to the righthand side of the cage, he noticed three of the rebar rods disconnected from the top edge of metal. He ran his hand along them, making them wobble slightly. "Dammit, I literally stepped away from the truck for… *thirty seconds.*"

"Do I need to call animal control?" Isabella had already pulled her phone out.

Drew hopped off the truck and looked over to people entering the zoo's East gate. "You're going to have to clear more than just the vet building."

FOUR

"I HAVE to say, once you've walked with dinosaurs, a modern-day zoo becomes kind of…meh." Kamren held his girlfriend's hand as they neared the 'Waterfowl Lagoon' in the south end.

"Walked?" After snapping a picture to catalog more of their trip on social media, Vivienne wore a slight scowl on her face. "You were *dragged* into a lake, I was chased by *Edward Scissorhands* dinosaurs, and E-A was…."

They slowed their stroll as the circumstances of their friend had been weighing on their minds for the last year and a half.

Emily-Ann had chosen to stay in prehistoric time with her father. Their love for science and discovery tipped the scale compared to living out the rest of their lives in a chaotic modern world.

Viv finally spoke again. "Wherever she is—"

"When, remember?" Kam added.

"Either way, I hope she and her dad are okay."

Kam stopped in front of her, broke his hand away from hers, and wrapped his arms around her. As her face nestled into his shoulder, he smiled and gently gave her neck a peck. "Considering Theo was able to train certain dinosaurs, I'd say they're more than capable of being okay."

Enjoying being in his caring embrace, Viv leaned back a tad. "True enough." Her peripheral vision helped her to spot a particular building a short walk away. "Hey, sorry, but I need a moment in the bathroom."

Kam smirked. "Oh, did I accidentally squeeze something out of you?"

Already out of his hug, she turned around and giggled. "Maybe. Check your leg."

His smirk immediately transitioned to shock. "Wait, what?" He held out each leg and checked over his jeans.

"Made you look!"

Once Viv had strolled far enough away, Kam took out his cellphone and called one of the recent contacts.

"Kammy-bo-bammy, how's the road trip going?" Arty Lancaster, Viv's little brother answered. "Are you in Chick-a-go right about now?"

"Sure are," Kam responded with a grin. Ever since he and Viv had become boyfriend and girlfriend, he'd appreciated that Arty had accepted him right away. "Just visiting one of the zoos right now."

"Ah, taking Viv back where she belongs."

"Well, when we're making out she can be an animal—"

"Blegh, come on man! That's *my sister* you're talking

about."

Kam let out a big laugh before replying. "Dude, you set me up for that."

"Aaaanyway…." Arty let a chuckle slip out. "Have you decided on the details of the *'you know what'?"*

Kam sighed as he scratched his cheek and leaned against a large planter. He took a quick glance over at the bathroom area, which told him Viv wasn't on her way back yet. "Honestly, Arty, it feels like I have writer's block, but the proposal version."

"I'm sure you'll figure it out." Arty paused for a moment. "You know, I'm all for you being my future-bro-in-law, but are you sure this isn't too soon?"

Giving in to his heart and head agreeing, he smiled. "She's been my best friend since forever. Who doesn't want to spend forever with their best friend?"

Within the bathroom stall, Viv had just started to finish up. Reaching for some toilet paper, she heard someone with boisterous laughter walking past the slightly ajar doorway. The noise echoed inside thanks to the tile and acoustics.

Viv tore off a piece of one-ply. "Useless."

Pit-pat-pit-pat-pit-pat.

She squinted at the noise of what seemed like little footsteps.

Pit-pat-pit-pat.

Uncertainty made her gaze dart from side to side. "Hello?"

Dooo-dooo.

The odd reply made Viv's scowl turn humorous. *Is this some kid?* "Uh…hi?"

Pit-pat-pit-pat-pit-pat.

Dooo-dooo!

From Viv's vantage point—still seated on the ceramic throne—she spied avian-like feet on the other side of the stall door. *A seagull… or big pigeon?*

Its yellowish feet shifted and pointed toward the stall.

Viv snorted. "Trust me, little guy, you *don't* want to come in—"

Dooo-dooooo!

"What the *heck?*"

Kam had finished the call with Arty and continued to wait. Although, by now, he realized she'd already taken a fair bit of time. Taking out his cellphone again, he began typing a text to her:

Did you fall in, or—

"Excuse me, folks." A zoo employee held up a bullhorn to make an announcement. Behind him, a team of half a dozen security began spreading out. "Hate to do this to you all, but a couple of small creatures have escaped their enclosures. We need everyone to please vacate the zoo, you will be given compensation at the gates."

"What? Really?" Kam shoved the phone back in his pant pocket as he half-jogged over to the bathroom area.

One of the zoo's security personnel approached, putting up a hand in denial. "Hey, kid, that means you, too."

Kam pointed to the door. "But my girlfriend's still in there."

"Gotcha." Nodding, the man took a step back and spoke into a walkie-talkie. "Reminder to check the bathrooms. The *creature* could be in any of those."

The security guard's little inflection on the word made Kam squint. "What escaped, exactly?"

The guard's expression remained stiff. "What matters is getting everyone to safety."

Their response made Kam rub his anxious hands together. "Thanks, Captain Vague."

Still, Viv hadn't exited the bathroom.

Every moment of her not coming out made Kam worry. *What if it already got to her? What if it slipped in while I was on the phone?* Subconsciously, his breathing sped up. *I need her.* He grabbed onto the doorknob, ready to rip the door off its hinges if need be.

"Whoa, jeez!" Viv finally stepped back outside and almost knocked into him. "Were you about to barge in?"

"I, uh…." Kam let go of the handle and repositioned his hand to her shoulder. "I was about to text you. You were in there for—"

"All right, folks," the security personnel waved them along. "Best be on your way now."

Taking the cue, the adolescents marched away from the

area.

"What took so long?" Kam snorted to himself. "Were you almost sacrificed to the toilet bowl gods or what?"

Viv stared straight ahead. "Kamren, we have to get back to the hotel room, *now.*"

Her use of his full name and urgency made him even more concerned. The last time he'd seen her this agitated, they'd been traversing a world with prehistoric creatures.

"Vivienne, what's going…"

Her arms cradled her stomach.

"…on? Wait, you're supposed to *lose* weight when you go to the bathroom—"

"Don't draw attention to it."

Kam glanced to it again.

Something within the fabric shuffled around.

"Seriously, Viv, are you *stealing* an—"

"Kam, *shut up* and *trust me.*"

He stopped walking for a second and did his best to pull all his fretting deep inside. She was one of the few people with whom trust would always be absolute.

By now, they'd come up to a gate at the southwest end of the zoo.

While other zoo-goers were up in arms about having to leave or get their money back, Viv blew right past everyone and over to a parked cab.

Kam opened the door for her, then hurried to the other side.

"Hotel Lincoln, please," Viv instructed the driver, trying to sound as calm as possible. It became awkward trying to slip the seatbelt on while keeping the creature tucked against her.

Kam shut the back passenger door and reached over. "Need a hand, m'lady?" Once he helped her clip it in, he readied himself as well.

The taxi driver pulled out from the parking spot.

Dooo-d—

"Oh God," Viv grabbed onto a section of the creature, as well as the fabric, and kept its mouth shut. "Jeez, um... Dooo-dooo, dooo-dooo-dooo."

Perplexed, the driver peeked into the backseat with the rear-view mirror.

"Mah nà mah nà," Kam continued, trying to help her with the ruse.

It continued for most of the ride, except for when the driver gave them extremely annoyed glares from the mirror.

Once they arrived at the hotel, they left a tip and rushed inside. Coming to the elevators, Kam pushed the button to go up. Thankfully, they only had to wait a few seconds until the arrival noise made its ding.

They embarked into the safety of the elevator.

As soon as the doors closed, Viv sighed. "I need a break."

Her cramping arms slackened.

The smuggled creature fell out from the hoodie and tumbled to the floor.

Feathers covered most of it.

Dooo-dooo.

"What the heck is...." The more Kam stared at it, the faster he pulled his phone out. He searched for what he figured it to be.

Results popped up on the screen.

Viv rubbed her biceps. "Is it what I think it is?"

A childish grin formed on his face as he compared the picture to what was standing right in front of him. "That's…a dodo bird?"

FIVE

"HOW IS there... I mean, I can kinda guess how." With his fingers interlaced behind his neck and arms bent at the sides of his head, a perplexed Kamren sat on the foot edge of the hotel bed. "But *why* was there a *dodo bird* at the zoo?"

The knee-high avian creature trotted over to Vivienne and stared up at her.

Dooo-dooo.

Kam grinned at the vocalization. "Kinda sounds like a pigeon."

"They've been extinct since sixteen-eighty-one," Viv recounted from the online article they'd read. "Did someone there do a successful cloning, or...."

Dooo-dooo-dooo.

Kam smiled at the mostly black and grey-feathered, inquisitive bird. "Maybe. Scientists are still trying with mammoths and things like that."

"Or is it a simpler explanation, because of what *we know.*

Like how Sebastian has his dinosaurs, how many more people took dinosaurs and whatever else from beyond the rifts? Did the dodo even come from the zoo, or was it lost?" Continuing to hypothesize in her mind, Viv took a few steps over to the bathroom door.

The dodo had to strut a little faster just to keep up with the human.

Kam smirked. "It seems to like you."

Viv came to a stop. "Huh—ow."

Fluttering its wings, the dodo had bumped into her calf. *Dooo-dooo-dooo.*

It rubbed the side of its feathery head up and down her leg, then cocked its head to look up at her.

Dooo-dooo.

"Yup, it's twitterpated all right," Kam chuckled, taking a picture with his phone. "Now, what to name it—"

"We are *not* getting attached to this thing," Viv yelled back, making the little bird twitch and stagger backward. "We just need to figure out what to do with it."

Kam stood up from the bed. "If you want nothing to do with it, then why did you take it from the zoo?"

"Because…." Flustered, she leaned against the corner wall just before the bathroom door. "Because it didn't belong there."

"No animal really belongs in a zoo."

"But this is different."

He raised an eyebrow. "Different because it's supposed to be extinct?"

"Yes, because it's *not* supposed to be *here* and *now,*" she countered with her voice raised even more. "If anyone else other than us had seen it, who knows what they would've done with it."

Smiling, he nodded. "So you *do care* about it."

"It's a helpless animal, Kam," she replied with crossed arms. "Jeez, give me a break—"

"Okay, okay, I'm sorry, Viv," he responded as he came over to her. He didn't want it to escalate into a debate or fight. They hadn't experienced their first fight yet. Although they had playfully debated over their road trip music playlist on occasion, it had never escalated. "We'll figure this out."

"I hope so…." She trailed off, glancing around the room. "Wait, where did it go?"

Turning to survey the hotel room, Kam stepped over to the opposite side of the room. "Maybe it's making a nest under the bed."

She rolled her eyes. "There's nothing here to make a nest with—"

Dooo-dooo.

An echo of its noise came from the bathroom.

Viv turned around and walked in. "Hey, what are—"

Dooo-doooooo.

The dodo had made it into the bathtub.

Kam entered right at the moment the bird tapped its beak on the faucet handle. "What's it doing in here?"

"I'm just trying to figure that out right now." Viv lowered herself to the bird's level, then placed her hand on the lever handle. "Do you want some water?"

A gushing of cold liquid came from the polished chrome

spout.

Angling its head to the side, the dodo opened its oblong beak and began taking sips. It ran its head under the controlled stream and flapped its wings before covering its entire body.

"Weird." Kam sat down on the side of the tub. "It's like it knew water came out of it."

"Maybe it could smell it," Viv theorized, impressed with the creature. "Pretty smart for a little dodo, huh?"

Dooo-dooo.

The bird quivered and kicked up droplets onto the two humans.

Viv wiped some off of her face. "Ugh, now I'm gonna smell like wet bird."

Already grabbing a couple small towels, Kam chuckled. "Sebastian would probably get a kick out of this thing."

She accepted one of the hand towels and started patting herself down. "Speaking of Sebastian, we should call him about this."

"Sure." Kam dabbed her cheek with his square of fabric before giving it a kiss. "I'll send you his number."

Smiling due to his lips on her skin, Viv gave him a surprised stare. "What, you want *me* to call him?"

"Oh no, talking to someone, *oh no!*" Kam left the bathroom and headed back to the bed. "You grabbed the dodo, therefore you get to call him."

Exasperation and regret mixed within Viv's sigh. "Fine." Less than a minute later, she had the phone number on her call screen and dialed.

"Sebastian Sharpe, who's this?"

"Hey, Seb, this is Viv, you're on speaker."

"Really?" Sebastian's smile came through in his tone. "How are you and Kamren?"

She scratched at her temples. "We're good."

Dooo-dooo.

By her feet, the dodo kept turning its head side to side to gaze up at her.

"Yeah, we're good."

Sebastian didn't even notice the noise. "It's nice to hear from you, I was actually just about to sit down for a late lunch—"

"So something happened today," Viv announced, getting right down to it. "Do you have any dinosaur business connections in Chicago?"

A thoughtful pause came from Sebastian. "Other than a couple of employees, why do you—"

"We found a dodo bird at the Lincoln Park Zoo."

Sebastian found himself in another moment of silence. "Really? A dodo bird?"

Kam spoke up. "Technically, *Viv* found it, and its name is Phrodo."

Viv turned around and glared at him. "Seriously, Kam?"

"Phrodo the dodo," he managed to respond while chuckling to himself. "It's small like a hobbit and it rhymes, but it has to be with a Ph because trademarks."

Dooo-dooo.

"See, it likes—"

"Anyway," Viv turned her attention back to the person

with more experience with extinct beings. "What should we do with it? Is there anything you can do?"

"I guess…" Sebastian worked through his options. "…I can call one of my contacts. I'll have them pick you up asap."

"Good," Kam piped up once more. "Because at the rate Phrodo is laying down bird-turds, the housekeeping bill is going to be prehistorical."

SIX

"DODO BIRD, huh?" Felicia Voorhees poked at a slice of radish in among her pickled beet and feta salad. She'd joined her colleague and boyfriend for lunch in their dining room. "How does one show up all of a sudden?"

"It's concerning." Sebastian dipped the end of his pizza crust into a small cup of spicy marinara. "All time rifts are supposed to be closed, and I don't recall any dodo's ever being acquired in the past."

She stared up at the white ceiling with wooden beams stretching from end to end. "Now I'm curious…." Opening her laptop, she waited for it to boot up in order to access old SauraCorps intel.

Finishing another morsel, Sebastian repositioned his chair to view her screen. "What are you thinking?"

"That maybe someone wasn't telling us everything," she responded along to the beat of her typing on the keyboard. Lists and manifests popped up. After scrolling for a second, she typed in the keyword 'dodo'.

NO ASSETS FOUND

"Has someone else been slipping creatures past security since the beginning?" Sebastian leaned back in his hand-crafted wooden chair. He let the last piece of pizza crust marinate in the dip as he shook his head. "First we catch the cartel smuggling dinosaurs for food, then those underground hatcheries, and we barely have any info on that bug collector. Where does it end?"

Felicia tried a couple more word searches only to come up with nothing. She sipped her tall glass of water. "Maybe... What if *he's back?*"

About to theorize in another direction, he halted at her guess. "Felicia, we've tried everything to link him to all of this. *Everything.*" Closing his tired eyes, he squeezed his eyelids shut at the thought. "If it even is him, he's doing a pretty fantastic job of covering it all up. There's no way to catch him."

"We'll think of something, Seb." She took his free hand and squeezed it with hers. "Cocky people can get their massive egos caught in the smallest of traps, one way or another."

Sebastian wore a disheartened grin before stuffing his face with the last bit of dressing-embalmed crust. "Hope so."

Felicia closed the laptop. "Okay, well, I was hoping to bring this up to you when you were in a good mood, but it can't be put off any longer." She gazed out the window to one of the glass domes housing multiple dinosaurs. "How much more do you intend to expand these enclosures?"

His arms folded together as his cheek muscles flexed.

"Seb, we're exceeding comfortable space for these dinosaurs," she continued, pointing a hand to the window for emphasis. "Don't get me wrong, I support everything you're doing here. We're keeping them alive and happy, which is great. As for resources and room, though, we're exhausting both."

"I know." He scratched at the stubble on his chin. Owning up to the circumstances was the first thing. Now it had become a matter of doing something about it. *The modern world isn't ready for dinosaurs.* "Wish I knew how to fix it."

The last bite of salad went down as Felicia wore a contemplative stare. "Maybe we could invest in some islands."

Sebastian snorted. "As long as we don't build a park for the public."

"Although, none of the dinosaurs would attack anyone," she countered with a playful grin. "You wouldn't even need electric fences."

"True, but that's still a no." Sebastian picked up his phone before making his way over to her. "I should call Beaumont to pick up Kam and Viv."

Felicia stood up and grabbed her bowl. "How much are you planning on telling them?"

"We'll see how it goes." He followed her lead and rose from his chair while dialing the dinosaur veterinarian.

Felicia snuck a kiss from his lips and headed off to tend

to other matters.

"Dr. Beaumont, hope I didn't catch you at a bad time," Sebastian began, looking out the window again to the dinosaurs roaming the property. "Keeping well?"

"Hey, Sebastian, things are a little hectic. How's everyone over there?"

"We're fine." He spotted Trudy his troodon friend socializing with her new pack and grinned. "Are you close to home, by chance?"

"Just about to head out, actually, why?"

"I'll be sending you an address. I need you to pick up some friends of mine and take them to your dino shelter." He turned his back to the view and settled onto the small ledge of window jamb. "They stumbled across a small *live package* I think you'll be interested in."

"Okay, I'll grab a crate. Do I need to take any precautions for it?"

"For the package, no you'll be fine." Sebastian's grin grew a little bigger. "But I hope you can handle teenagers."

SEVEN

DOWN IN the underground parking, Kamren and Vivienne waited for their ride near his truck. A makeshift leash had been formed out of one of Kam's belts, which he held onto to keep Phrodo close by.

"Gotta say, I'd been wondering about what happens now that dinosaurs are still technically here in our present," Kam brought up as he watched the dodo bird pacing around. "Seb's got his dino-preserve, but who knows what else is out there."

Viv had been sitting up on the tailgate for the past ten minutes and hadn't said much. "Yup, who knows."

Although the dodo had kept his attention a fair bit, Kam picked up on her distant tone. "Viv, are you okay?"

In response, she closed her eyes and gripped the edge of the tailgate. "I'll be fine."

Kam squinted at her. *Which usually means she's not fine.* He stepped closer to her and slouched forward to catch her gaze. "What's going on, sweet pea?"

A quick glance into his caring eyes made her avert her gaze to the left. "Our trip has been put on hold for a bird."

Dooo-dooo.

Kam looked over at Phrodo, who had discovered a side mirror of a small car beside them. It tried to call to what it didn't understand to be its reflection. When a response didn't come, it pecked at the mirror.

"A minor hiccup." Kam shrugged, hoping to keep her spirits up. "Once we hand Phrodo over to Seb's friend, we can carry on our merry way—" His cellphone sang its indie tune of *Worlds on Fire* by Zerbin, and he bopped his head as he answered. "Wham bam, this is Kam."

"Uh… Hi." Beaumont paused at the teenager's odd introduction. "I'm Sebastian's contact and I'm sitting out front in a black mini-van."

"Awesome, we'll be right out."

Not far from the parking lot's exit onto the main street, Kam and Viv made it out within a minute. To not bring any attention to themselves, Viv had resorted back to carrying Phrodo within Kam's hoodie.

"There's the van," Kam pointed out, making his way over to it.

Beaumont spotted the nineteen-year-olds from the driver side window and hopped out to meet them. "Are you Kamren and Vivienne?"

"That we are." He smiled while holding out his hand. "And you are?"

"Dr. Dawn Beaumont," she replied in a friendly yet

professional fashion. "I've worked with Sebastian since SauraCorps began." More excited to meet the mystery animal, she glanced around in anticipation. "Where's the *package?*"

Dooo-dooo.

Dawn set her eyes on the girl's unusually bulky hoodie and smirked. "Is it…in there?"

Viv nodded and grinned. "I think it's starting to like being in here, actually."

The veterinarian rushed over and opened the back door of her van. "Bring it over here, we can keep it out of everyone's view."

Following instructions, Viv came up to the bumper. "All right, Phrodo, you're going to go with this nice lady now, okay?"

Phrodo poked its black-feathered head out from under the hoodie. It noted the simple crate in the back of the van as a smaller version of its earlier prison.

In awe, Dr. Beaumont brought a hand to her mouth. "You have a *dodo bird?*"

Dooo-dooo-dooo!

Viv lost control of the dodo bird as it fluttered and wriggled free. She lurched forward to try and get a handle on it. "Come here, you—agh, no!"

Dodging Viv's arms, the bird launched itself off the bumper, and landed in the busy street.

SCREEEECH!

A sportscar managed to brake inches from the darting dodo.

Phrodo cocked its head, pecked twice at the shiny front bumper, and carried on.

Beaumont reached into the back of her van. "Go after it, I'll get the net!"

"Awesome." Kam stepped foot onto the asphalt. "Frogger with a dodo."

Phrodo almost made it to the next lane when a pick-up truck raced past. Pulling its head back at the last second, it glanced back at the oncoming humans.

Other drivers had stopped their vehicles, poking their arms out of windows while shouting their confusion and frustrations.

Viv saw the bird turn left and weaved behind an idle taxi. "Come on, Phrodo." She thrust her arms out to try and catch it. "We're just trying to—"

HOOOOOOOONK!

Phrodo jumped at the obnoxious car noise and bolted the opposite direction.

Kam stepped into the dodo's path. "Got you—*whoa!*"

Phrodo bobbed its head side to side like a tiny football player before careening right.

Crouching into a tumble to the asphalt, Kam nearly scraped his hands. "Jeez, it's like Phrodo's protecting a ring or something."

The dodo hopped up onto the hood of a small vehicle, scaring the woman behind the wheel into honking her horn. Agitated, Phrodo waddled up the windshield to the car's roof and flapped its small wings.

"Come on, birdie," Beaumont spoke as she approached

37

with her long-handled net. "We need to take you somewhere safe."

With one eye on the veterinarian, Phrodo noticed Kam and Viv sneaking up from other angles. Surrounded by humans, the bird hesitated while calling out in distress.

WHUMP!

Net ensnared the prehistoric creature.

"Gotcha." Beaumont worked fast to maneuver her arms around it to keep the bird from jumping back out. Sweeping the netting across the top of the car, she managed to flip the bag-like net over. "Give me a hand, kids. Don't want a repeat of what just happened."

Traffic returned to normal as they all made their way over to the sidewalk.

The back door to the van had been left open, which made it easy for Dr. Beaumont to prepare to place the dodo in the crate. Once both teens stood on either side of her to block another attempted escape, she flipped the net again and gently released the dodo.

More cries came from the bird.

Kam glanced around at the curious bystanders. "Looks like people are getting ready to post to *TikTok*."

"Watch yourselves." Beaumont slammed the door closed, then hurried to the driver seat. "Climb in, we'll get Sebastian to take care of it."

Viv grabbed onto the handle of the sliding door. *Of all the things to happen.* Her reflection showed her just how much she didn't want to get involved.

Knock-knock.

Kam leaned over and looked up at her through the tinted window. "There's no candy in here, but come on in."

Viv allowed a slight smirk to form while opening the door. "No candy? What?"

"You know, strangers with candy in their vans," Kam answered with a silly grin, then looked ahead at the veterinarian. "Unless you do have some, which I'm totally cool with."

Beaumont rolled her eyes. "There might be some mints in the console."

Viv clipped the seatbelt into place. "Are they magical mints that will wake me up from this dream?"

Dooo-dooo.

Phrodo snapped the crate's lock mechanism with the curved tip of its beak. It scrambled out, squeezed itself between the middle seats, and hopped up into Viv's lap. As if it had done nothing wrong, it gazed up at her.

Dooo-dooo.

Amazed, Beaumont unclipped her seatbelt to turn around slightly. "Did that thing just—"

"It's a surprisingly smart bird," Kam stated, holding back a chuckle. "Looks like you have your own version of Nandy, Viv."

"Great." Viv had her hands up in the air, but eventually let them rest onto the prehistoric bird. "I've always wanted a dodo."

EIGHT

HERMOSILLO, MEXICO

ROARS OF planes filled the atmosphere of the Hermosillo International Airport. Incoming and outgoing travelers remained oblivious to two groups meeting together on a back road northwest of the airport.

Approaching from the west, two modified dump trucks outfitted with armor came to a creaking, ominous stop.

About a hundred feet away, a group of suited people stood in front of four escalades.

"Of course, they brought their narco-tanks," one of the men in suits mentioned loud enough for the whole group to hear. "Stay on alert."

The guy beside him remained stoic. "An intimidation tactic."

A passenger door to one of the tanks opened.

In the hands of its owner, the barrel of a semi-automatic

rifle showed itself first. A member of the Sinaloa cartel poked his head out. Once he'd surveyed the environment, he spoke in Spanish to the rest of his buddies.

More men and guns disembarked from the armored vehicles.

The stoic American swallowed down a hard lump. "The tactic is working."

Letting the rifle hang at his side, the first cartel member stepped forward. "Our boss appreciates your doing business with us." He pointed to the extra-wide transport truck behind the suited men and their escalades. "Is that our delivery?"

Standing the closest to them, the responding man nodded. "Keys are in the ignition."

Half a dozen of the cartel marched forward, following their appointed executor of this business deal. Two in the back carried briefcases of money.

The cartel's leading member scratched at his trimmed beard. "It is alive, *si?*"

"Alive and tranquilized."

A smirk appeared on his face. "We'll need some proof, *amigo.*"

Confusion took over most of the opposite group.

"We don't recommend that unless it's in a secure—"

"This is our first deal," the Mexican countered. "Let us make sure it's not dead, or else you and your friends will *not* be flying home."

The group of sellers glanced at each other, making a collective decision by their facial expressions. They all

knew not to mess with the cartel. Plus, future deals were
on the line.

"I said it's alive and tranq'd. Follow us."

Half of the cartel group remained with the narco-tanks as
the others were led to the back end of the transport truck.
They all wore skeptical glares as the large white doors swung
open to reveal the package.

An adolescent ankylosaurus laid on the bed of the truck.
Heavy-duty chains had been thrown over the armored
dinosaur and were hooked into the metal flooring.

It didn't move. Not even a twitch.

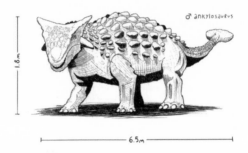

"Now to make sure it isn't dead." The cartel member
pulled out an insulated rod and pressed a button on the
lower shaft.

Prongs shot out with an electric crackle.

Alarmed, the main seller reached for a concealed
handgun. "Wait, what the heck are you—"

Z-Z-Z-ZAP!

Unable to pull the bearded man away from the truck
fast enough, another from the selling team yelled out, "You
friggin' idiot."

MMMMRRRRUUUUAAAAWW!

Waking from its deep tranquilizer slumber, the ankylosaur opened its eyes and panicked due to its strange new environment.

"Close the doors!" someone called out, which prompted others to do so. "Keep it confined while we figure out what to do—"

SMASH!

A partition of the truck's metal siding bulged outward.

"—with it."

Over by the narco-tanks, the other men murmured in Spanish as the transport rocked side to side. Some crossed themselves before readying their weapons.

Pops from the chains mimicked gunshots from within the transport.

The ankylosaurus wailed once more.

WHA-BANG!

Its clubbed tail made impact with the other side.

Stun baton still in hand, the cartel group leader backed away. *"Dios mio."*

Infuriated, the seller marched after him. "Great job, *Nacho Libre.* Better help us take this thing on, and bullets *barely do anything* to it."

Every thrash of the ankylosaurus' tail and body weakened the metal siding even more. Rivets popped out like bullets as the dinosaur's head spikes poked through.

"This thing's like an armored bull." The seller held up his gun. "Aim for the underbelly if you ca—"

Both doors on the back of the truck flew open.

MMRRAAAAUUUUWW!

The ankylosaurus charged, tumbling to the ground. Nearly twice the size of one of the escalades, its bulk didn't hinder its agility as it stood up and snorted in aggravation.

"Fuego!"

Everyone understood the Spanish and began firing at the prehistoric beast.

Bullets ricocheted off the creature's thick hide as it spun around, surveying its unfamiliar attackers. It charged forward, just missing one of the men with its head. A swift flick of its tail knocked another human off his feet.

The two narco-tanks took off toward the dinosaur.

Still enraged by the barrage of ammo deflecting off its hide, the ankylosaurus noticed the incoming hefty vehicles.

One of the drivers kept his foot pressed against the gas pedal.

The ankylosaurus didn't back down.

It rushed directly at one of the narco-tanks, braced its front feet into the ground, and used the momentum to swing its back end toward the attackers.

CRUNCH-BAM!

Its clubbed tail collided with the front driver's side, smashing off the metal protection and popping the wheel off.

Unable to control their trajectory, the driver couldn't fight the lean of the vehicle as it crashed into the second narco-tank.

MMRRAAAAUUUUWW!

Done with being assaulted, the ankylosaurus fled the

scene as more bullets pelted off of its solid exterior.

"Dammit." The seller hopped into one of the escalades and pulled out his cellphone. "The boss won't like this."

NINE

KAMREN AND Vivienne entered the veterinarian's home and sat at the kitchen island. On the southern outskirts of cityscapes, Dr. Beaumont's farmhouse took in a fair bit of property.

"Would either of you like something to drink?" Dawn let the dodo run free while she went into hospitable mode. "I've got water, iced tea... Sorry, I don't have soda."

"I'll have some water, please." Viv stared at the island countertop while picking at her left thumb.

"No soda? That's a travesty," Kam commented with sarcasm. "Iced tea is fine, thank you."

Dawn Beaumont had grabbed a metal bowl and filled it up with water. She set it down on her tiled floor for Phrodo, who strutted over and began dipping its beak into the cool liquid. Beaumont then sent a message on her phone before serving the kids their drinks.

Kam took a generous sip of his iced tea. "Do you keep

any dinosaurs out here on your farm?"

"If it's a smaller one, sometimes I let it stay inside with me," Dawn answered while pouring herself some water. "The odd time, I'll let one stay out in the barn. It's not always easy explaining the weird sounds to some of the neighbors, though."

Viv looked up from mutilating her cuticles. "Weird sounds?"

Dawn chuckled to herself. "Some dinosaurs can get a little vocal in the evenings, especially parasaurolophus. Or if they get hungry, even baby rexes can whine pretty good."

Kam almost choked on his drink. "You've had a baby T-rex here?"

"Yeah, the poor thing appeared on my property about a year ago when the rifts went crazy," Dawn explained while replaying the event in her mind. "One of them opened up right inside my barn, and the little guy came crashing through."

"We were on the prehistoric side of that rift craziness." Kam nodded as he spoke, then looked over at his girlfriend. "We didn't know if making it home was possible at that point."

Viv reached over and took one of his hands. "Thankfully, we did. Hopefully, we *never* have to go through that *ever* again."

Dawn's phone buzzed. She read the message, then grabbed her laptop and opened it. "Sebastian's ready for a video chat." Once she'd signed into her device and plugged in the chat info, they connected to the secure virtual room.

Sebastian's face popped up with the ambiance of his office behind him. "Hey, nice to see everyone's faces again."

"Mr. Sebastian, looking *Sharpe* as always," Kam responded with a smirk.

Viv snorted, rolled her eyes, and smacked her boyfriend's arm. "Hardy-har. Good to see you, Seb."

"Same to you, Viv." The businessman turned his attention to his employee. "Dr. Beaumont, always a pleasure. How's the dodo bird?"

Dawn picked up the creature and tucked it under her right arm. "Other than giving us a runaround in a busy street, Phrodo seems to be in good health and temperament."

"Which reminds me, should we be worried about people filming us with their phones?" Viv brought up, concerned for her safety.

Sebastian leaned his head side to side. "Leave it with me. If it blows up, we'll make it seem like a runaway turkey and then it'll be yesterday's news."

Kam snorted. "Gotta love media manipulation."

"SauraCorps was successful with it in the past," Sebastian noted, though slight guilt entered his tone. "Now that I'm at the helm, it's to keep both the public and dinosaurs safe."

"I remember San Francisco was a doozy, though," Dawn mentioned, setting the dodo down as she remembered the news footage. A block-wide rift had sent multiple vehicles and people into the prehistoric world's clutches. "Those poor people."

"And we're still doing everything we can to help those families," Sebastian spoke with solemn empathy.

Dooo-dooo.

Phrodo flapped its wings and prodded Viv's leg with its beak.

Viv gazed down at the bird and sighed. "What's the matter?"

The bird tried to hop up and place its beak in her lap.

"You want up?"

Dooo-dooo-dooo.

Kam laughed at the creature. "I love how it actually thinks it can talk to us."

Once Viv lugged Phrodo up onto her lap, she made sure to lock eyes with it. "If you poop on me, you're back on the floor. Understand?"

Phrodo cocked its head back and forth as if it processed her instructions.

Viv held up an index finger. "Got it?"

Dooo-dooo.

"Good."

On the laptop screen, Sebastian grinned, in awe of the new creature. "Right, I guess it's time we discuss some things about…Phrodo, you call it?"

Kam raised an eyebrow. "As long as you emphasize the P-h."

Sebastian made a confused face for a moment before continuing. "Okay…. Anyway, is there anything at all within the events of finding…Phrodo…that would be of major significance? And I mean *anything*. It could really help us with…a certain situation."

Chuckling to himself, Kam began. "Viv was taking a—"

"Dude!" Viv smacked him harder than previous times. "I was in the bathroom, minding my own business—"

"Ha, *business,*" Kam quipped.

Again, Viv whipped her hand at his shoulder, which prompted Phrodo to peck him in the deltoid to help in chastising him. She giggled while patting the bird on its head. "Good job, Phrodo. But yeah, no one came in the bathroom except this little guy who waddled in."

Sebastian's eyebrows scrunched together. "Oh, that's it? You didn't see anyone, in particular, running after it?"

Shaking his head, Kam added, "I was outside on the phone, but I didn't see anyone looking sketchy. Zoo personnel was all over the place telling everyone to leave because of an escaped animal."

Dawn finally piped up, "Wait, so *they knew* they needed to find something?"

"That's how they're doing it," Sebastian remarked, his eyelids flashing open as he leaned back in his chair. "The zoos. They're so unassuming."

"It makes sense, though," Dawn added, also working things out in her head.

Intrigued by the new SauraCorps owner's breakthrough, Kam leaned forward. "Should we be concerned about zoos now?"

Sebastian chewed on the inside of his cheek before replying. "I trust you two, so what I'm about to say *cannot* leave this room." He studied the nineteen-year-olds' faces for their compliance.

Viv braced herself. When she'd begun the road trip

across the country, the last thing she expected to be doing was holding a dodo bird while learning more about the situation of dinosaurs in present day. *I just want to enjoy my trip with—*

"Juicy deets?" Kam's voice overflowed with excitement. "Count us in!"

A small grimace showed up on Viv's face for a split second.

Resting his elbows on his desk and with his fingers interlaced in front of him, Sebastian began, "I believe I've mentioned before the man who used to live in the house I'm in now. He built his empire by dealing dinosaurs to anyone he wanted to, no questions asked. They were sold for food, black market commodity, and possibly more. Greed had blinded him beyond considering any consequences." Sebastian paused, closing his eyes as he recalled how he used to be in the beginning with SauraCorps. "After the main rift imploded, we have no idea of what happened to Bartelloni."

Kam snorted. "Sounds like some kind of pasta."

Viv shook her head as she added, "And sounds like he needed to meet some giant millipedes."

A chuckle escaped Sebastian's mouth. "Thing is, Bartelloni wasn't the only one committing criminal acts. We've successfully taken down some groups here and there, but we never could link them to a kingpin supplier." He tapped an index finger onto his desk. "With what you just told me, it makes sense that the zoos—possibly around the world—are being used for illegal dinosaur trade."

"Whoa, a dinosaur kingpin," Kam remarked, equally

fascinated and unsettled. "That would make a crazy book idea."

As distant as she wanted to be from all of it, Viv couldn't help getting curious. "Do you even know who that could be?"

"Sadly, yes," Sebastian answered as he scratched at his stubble. "And he's an ex-SauraCorps board member."

Dooo-dooo-dooooo.

Kam busted a gut as the dodo bird hopped off his girlfriend's lap. "That thing's…comedic timing…is impeccable."

Sebastian managed a grin before continuing. "His name is Blake Arrowsmith, and Felicia and I have reason to believe he's out of hiding once more. We don't know how or where he ghosts to, but that dodo bird is clear evidence that he's still operational."

"Wait, you mean like, *Aerosmith*, the band?" Kam chuckled as a playlist of songs popped in his head. "So would you say he's…*'Back in the Saddle'*?"

Sebastian squinted at his laptop's built-in webcam. "No, Arrowsmith as in bow and arrow—that's not important right now."

Dawn crossed her arms as she began pacing. "We just need to figure out some way of catching him or his people."

Meanwhile, on the other side of the island, Phrodo hopped to try and snag an apple from the edge of a fruit bowl.

"Are you hungry?" Viv stood up to go help it. "Didn't think you'd be interested in fruit."

As she turned the corner, she noticed the dodo bird eyeing up a drawer handle.

Phrodo hooked its beak onto the metal handle and flicked its head back.

The wooden-faced drawer rolled outward a tad.

Dooo-dooo.

Another attempt with its beak allowed Phrodo to open the drawer fully. It jumped up and used it to hop once more, allowing it to knock the apple to the tile floor. Phrodo followed the fruit until it stopped rolling, then struck the apple's flesh with its beak until a piece broke off.

Impressed with the creature, Viv grinned. "Man, I'm never calling anyone a dodo ever again. They're so smart!"

Kam studied the bird, then stared back at the laptop screen and spoke with full conviction. "We should return the dodo to the zoo."

A buzz of shock traveled through Viv's body. *"We?"*

Nodding to himself, Kam continued. "They clearly wanted the dodo, so let's give it back. Maybe while we're there, we can sneak around to see if we can find anything."

Dawn stopped pacing, impressed by the young man's suggestion. "That...could actually work. I can be an extra set of eyes and protection, plus I know a bit about their facilities."

Frozen in place on the other side of the kitchen island, Viv rubbed her face. "Kam, remember what happened *the last time* we tried to sneak in somewhere?" Her hands subconsciously moved to her stomach, trying to calm the anxious boulder within it. "What if they come after us?"

"Returning Phrodo will be like taking a lost dog back to its owner. We'd look completely innocent" Kam countered, eager to assist the refined SauraCorps in any way he could. "If we can give Dawn the opportunity to poke around— maybe by causing a diversion—it could give her ample time to try to find something."

Something churned in Viv's stomach as she went to open her mouth. "Kam, I—"

"Arrowsmith or his people definitely wouldn't expect you two," Sebastian added, liking the spontaneous plan. "It would still be dangerous. Dawn is one of my most trusted friends, but I don't want to force you into anything you don't want to do." He stared down at his keyboard and placed a hand over his mouth as he sighed. "Unfortunately, I'm getting desperate to stop Arrowsmith, so as long as you understand the risks, I would appreciate any help I can get."

Viv's arms slackened. *If I say no, will it make me sound like a jerk?* Her eyes focused on the grout between the tiles in the floor.

"We can do it tomorrow," Kam suggested as his grin morphed into more of a smirk. "I have one question about Arrowsmith, though."

Sebastian raised an eyebrow. "And that is?"

"Does this *'Dude' look like a lady?*"

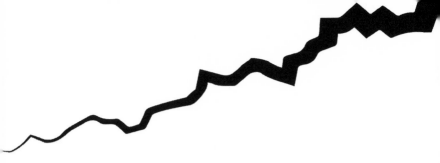

TEN

ONCE THE plan's details had been ironed out, Dr. Beaumont drove the teenagers back to their hotel. Everyone needed their rest before heading to the zoo the next day.

Kamren and Vivienne had left Phrodo with the veterinarian so they could enjoy their evening together. They'd made reservations for a fancy dinner, and had brought clothing especially for it.

In the bathroom, Viv had finished her makeup. Though physically ready, emotionally, she needed to give herself a pep-talk. *If he starts talking dino stuff, try to change the subject. Tonight is about us. Us. This whole trip was supposed to be about us.* Not *dinosaurs.* She gave herself a once-over, then closed her eyes. *I still love him.*

Meanwhile, as Kam finished tying his black and white striped necktie, he stared out the eighth-floor hotel window. The busy street sat down below, and across the way, other hotel walls with windows took up the view.

The day's events rolled through his mind, and by the end of them, only one question lingered. *How much has SauraCorps changed our world?* As he put together a list of the changes only him and Viv would've been aware of, he sat on the edge of the bed. *What can I do to help fix—*

"Don't you look snazzy."

Kam turned around and his jaw released. "Whoa... Lady Lancaster, you look absolutely magnificent."

"Oh, stop it." Viv blushed, as his compliment seeped in. Every step she took made the floor-length silvery dress shimmer around her. She didn't get many opportunities to dress up, but she'd been looking forward to wearing something fancy for their night out. "You on the other hand..." She worked her hands up his necktie, pulling both of them closer to each other in the process. "...need to wear suits more often, like prom night."

"Is that so?" He angled his head to the side as their foreheads nearly touched. The silky dress made her glow in a way he'd never seen before, giving him nerves he couldn't fully process. "I could suit more wears—I mean, *wear* more *suits,* if you'd like."

She leaned in, letting her nose brush against his as she giggled at his word fluster. "Am I making you... overwhelmed?"

"You're definitely not making me whelmed," he responded, a jitter in his voice.

"Would you consider..." Viv grazed his upper lip with her bottom one. "...making out as an appetizer before dinner?"

Kam closed his eyes, ready to take her in his arms and

give her the most earth-shattering kiss ever. "Is it on…the secret menu?"

"Let's go down and see."

Viv's voice sounded further away.

By the time Kam opened his eyes, he found her standing by the door.

She wore a cheeky grin while stuffing one of the room's key cards in her handbag. "Aren't you coming?"

"Damn, girl, why you gotta tease me like that?"

"Because you're adorable when you're flustered."

A little later down in the hotel's restaurant, Kam and Viv were enjoying their meals. Not yet the legal drinking age of twenty-one, they had splurged on different mocktails. They'd also decided to split two of the entrees: a prime New York strip steak, and house-made potato gnocchi in a basil pesto.

Vivienne savored her bite of the Italian dumpling glistening with sauce. "This gnocchi is just… No words. There are *no words* for this meal."

To her left, Kamren popped another bite of steak in his mouth. "Culinary *perfection*. I would kiss the chef if I could."

"Hey." She scrunched her nose at the thought. "Trying to make me jealous or something?"

"On the cheek, sweet pea," he added to his statement along with a chuckle. "Both cheeks if they're European."

Wearing a teasing smirk, she squinted at him. "Uh huh."

Kam set down his fork and took her hand. "Vivienne, how could I ever make you jealous? You're the heart of my world and the atmosphere that surrounds me."

Viv lowered her glass of sangria. "Getting all mushy on me now?"

"I mean it, Vivienne."

His use of her full name and the warm sincerity of his tone made her heart flutter. She'd been enjoying the transition from having him as a best friend to being her boyfriend. Some days, though, she wished their romantic connection hadn't taken true form during the prehistoric era and under so much stress. The lingering anxiety of nearly losing one another had almost been too much to deal with. "I don't know how to be all artsy-fartsy with my words like you can, but I feel the same way."

Kam patted his hand against his lower jacket pocket. He'd brought the little black box just in case he had a good opportunity. "The more I think about it, you're more than both of those things combined. You're my universe."

Viv figured her entire face had turned a shade of pink. "Kamren, what's gotten into…." Her gaze traveled past him.

Someone from across the dining room stopped staring at them and sipped their beer to seem inconspicuous.

"Viv?" Kam waved his hand through her field of vision. "Dinner date to Viv, come in Vi—"

"There's some weirdo over there," she responded through clenched teeth, hoping to not bring any unwanted attention their way. "Pretty sure he's been *watching* us."

"Watching?" Kam changed tracks in his mind as the night seemed to be going in a different direction. He peered over and noticed the man take another brief glance. Disappointed, Kam sighed internally. *Why this night of all nights?* He took a shaky sip of his drink. "Maybe he just looks scary all the time, you know, resting-creep-face."

Viv managed a little snort at the term. "He's definitely giving off those vibes." Taking their day into consideration, she took a pensive pause. "What if he works for the Arrowsmith person?"

A shockwave of dread coursed through Kam. Rather than show his fear, he cleared his throat. "Maybe his name is Janie and he's got a gun."

"Dude, you need to stop with the Aerosmith jokes." Viv leaned over and smacked his arm. "Besides, you weren't even alive for their greatest hits."

"My parents were, though." He wore an amused grin. "They taught me their jedi-music ways."

"Uh huh, sure thing Master Eckhardt." She finished off her mocktail and glanced around the room. "Let's get the waiter's attention so we can leave."

The whole way to their hotel room, they made sure to keep an eye out for anyone who might have followed them. As far as they knew, the man from the restaurant hadn't tailed them. Swirling concerns took center stage in both of their heads.

Kamren tapped his fingers against the little black box in his suit pocket. *I wanted it to be tonight. Now she's going to be all worried about other things.* He gave his head a minor shake before tapping his key card to the reader, then opened the door for his girlfriend.

Not even crossing the threshold into their room gave Viv a sense of protection. She'd nibbled on the inside of her cheek and picked at one of her thumb's cuticles since they left the table downstairs. *If Arrowsmith is the dinosaur black market kingpin, a little hotel lock isn't going to stop him. That guy had to be his spy.* She started glancing all around the room. *What if this place is bugged? I can't handle—*

Music pulled her out of her downward spiral.

One of her current favorite songs flowed from the small speakers of Kam's cellphone: *Your Love is My Home* by The Light the Heat.

"Lady Lancaster," Kam held his right hand out to her, "Come hither."

She squinted at him, though couldn't keep a small smile off her face. "What are you—"

"Dance with me."

Taking his hand, she gave him an anxious stare. "Kam, this isn't—"

"Vivienne, *please,*" he implored, a blend of tenderness and nerves in his voice. "This is *nowhere near* the way I wanted this night to go."

She obliged him, taken by a subtle hurt in his tone. Part of her wondered if the guy down in the restaurant wasn't even a concern in the first place. "I didn't mean to ruin our night."

"It isn't ruined." Kam led in their swaying to the song. "You and me, right here and right now, this will always be perfect."

A single tear trickled down Viv's cheek as she set her head on his shoulder. Her frustration toward his desire of stepping back into a world she'd wanted to move on from wrestled with falling for this loving, sensitive moment he'd created.

"Tonight, it's all about you and me," he cooed, keeping his tone suave and reassuring. "As for tomorrow, we're going to *Mission: Impossible* the crap out of it."

She'd been close to getting herself under control until he brought up the next day. Rather than spit something negative back at him, she opted to tease. "Trying to make yourself sound like Tom Cruise?"

"Heck no," Kam laughed in reply. "Your Lara Croft moves with that millipede proved you're more like Cruise, which…I guess makes me Ving Rhames."

Viv chuckled at his actor comparisons. "Mhmm, you know that's right." After giving him a squeeze, she yawned as she stepped away. "This crazy day has me emotionally exhausted. We should finish eating, then just cuddle until we conk out."

About to say something, Kam closed his mouth and nodded. He figured her mind wasn't in the right frame for what he'd been dying to say to her. *Guess it won't be tonight then.* Removing their boxed-up food from the mini-fridge, he brought it over to their hotel bed. "As you wish."

ELEVEN

EARLY THE next morning, Vivienne woke to her Spotify playlist. She would usually wake up before the custom alarm could even start playing. Though it randomized, it seemed to favor *Dancing in the Street* by Stephen Day lately.

Turning over, she found Kamren on his side and facing away from her. Deciding on letting him sleep, she automatically started her morning routine.

She leaned her head side to side. The tension in her neck gave way to a couple of cracks. Her arms raised into the air to help in stretching out her back. Her legs barely dangled from the edge of the bed.

She let herself slide out and onto the thin carpet.

Crunch!

Her heel had struck something.

Sleepiness still filled most of her mind. *Did we…leave food on the floor?*

Gazing down, she lifted her foot.

A smushed millipede.

"Fricking *gross!*"

She leaped back onto the bed, which jostled Kam into being awake.

"Vi.... Viv?" He righted himself into a sitting position. "What's wrong?"

"On the floor," she blurted out while wiping her foot clean of any bug bits. "It's a damn millipede."

Kam raced into the bathroom to grab something to clean it up. "I'll get it."

Once she'd made sure her heel had been cleaned, she noticed a difference in color coming through the window to their room. She turned her gaze to the right.

Prehistoric treetops.

"How in the heck?" Uneasy steps brought her closer to the view. "Did the whole hotel get time rifted?"

A massive reptilian head rose from below, bringing its menacing eye level with hers.

She backed away even slower than before. "Oh…my… Go—"

RRRROOOOOOOOOOOOAAAAAAAAAARRRR!

Viv screamed in tandem with the Giganotosaurus. The entire room shook, and she worried the thick glass would shatter from the piercing bellow.

She hurried and slammed the bathroom door closed behind her, figuring she'd be far enough away from the raging dinosaur.

Catching her breath, she glanced around.

"K-Kam?"

The lack of response told her he wasn't in there.

"Kam?" Her throat tightened, making it harder to call out for him. "Ka... Kam, where...."

Uncontrollable sobs sent her leaning over the sink. Tears dripped from her cheeks to the drain. "Kam, I... *I need... you.*"

Something light tapped her on the back.

Wiping her face clear of waterworks, she looked up through the mirror.

Hiiiisssssssssss!

An oversized millipede twitched its mandibles inches away from her face.

Viv backed up into the door and scrambled for the handle. "No, no, God *noooooooo!*"

"Vivienne!"

Whipping bed sheets off of her, Viv woke to Kam sitting up beside her. "No... Wha-what?"

"Viv, you were having a nightmare," he stated with a concerned yet caring tone as he shuffled over to slip his arms around her. "You're okay, Viv. It's all okay."

Though one of his arms had pulled her head into his chest, she made sure to look over at the window.

Buildings lined the street on the other side.

No sign of any dinosaur.

The longer he held her, the easier it became for her to breathe. Among everything in her dream, the only part that crossed over into reality were the tears on her cheeks.

"I'm right here." Kamren kissed the top of her head and didn't care if some of her hairs stuck to his lips. "You're okay."

Half an hour later, they were finishing up their continental breakfast—which Kam had asked to be delivered—inside their room.

Mostly silent, Viv had let her phone's indie playlist fill their environment.

Kam popped the last bite of bacon into his mouth. Having her full-on jolting and whimpering beside him earlier in bed made him concerned for her emotional and mental well-being. "Vivienne, was that the first time you've had nightmares like that?"

She stared at the floor while the acidity of orange juice awakened her palate even more. His question had registered in her mind. Strands of her hair swayed as she shook her head in a distressed and shameful 'no' formation.

"And...you never wanted to tell me about them?" Being as sensitive as possible, he wished she would look him in the eyes. "Not...once?"

"I...." Viv had subconsciously bunched up a section of the bed's duvet in her left hand. "Believe me, you're the only one I've wanted to tell, but...."

Since her left hand was closest to him, he placed his right hand on top of it. "It's okay, sweet pea. Your heart is important to me, even when it's hurting."

For a split-second, she gazed into his loving eyes and forced a grin. "I didn't...." All throughout her life, he'd always been there for her. She'd always cherished their past moments when he'd given comfort with his arms wrapped around her, letting her sob by his side. She sucked in a deep breath, then huffed it out. "I didn't want to worry you."

"That's what I'm here for." Reassurance oozed from his voice. "Hardships and triumphs are more meaningful when shared with those you love."

His loving tone gave her more strength to look up at him. "There you go being all mushy—"

Kam pressed his lips into hers and slid his hand behind her head. Where words couldn't make a full impact, he made sure his actions filled in the cracks.

She kissed him back as a grin made its way onto her face. On coming out of the kiss, she sighed with delight. "Your words are even better when they're coated in bacon grease."

Kam's snort transitioned into a chuckle as he leaned back toward her. "Oh, so you want more of this, huh?"

"Ew," she countered, picking up a napkin and tossing it at him. "Wipe your face before you come at me with those again."

Buzzzz. Buzzzz.

Kam closed his eyes in defeat. As he slid over to his bedside table, he noted the name trying to contact him. "It's Sebastian. Must be the signal that Dr. Beaumont's waiting for us."

As Kam took the phone call, Viv returned her gaze to the carpeted floor. Getting through the day's plan continued to be her main goal. *Cause a distraction. Get in, get out.*

She nodded to herself as she added one more part of her own.

And then we'll stay out.

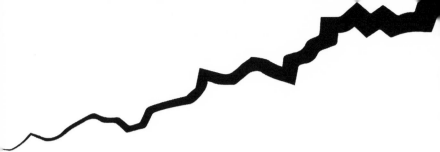

TWELVE

THE FAMILIAR minivan pulled up outside of the hotel.

Dr. Beaumont rolled down her window to make sure they recognized her.

Kamren held the hotel's front door open for Vivienne. Nerves and exhilaration jumbled together inside of him as he marched over to the vehicle.

Beside him, Viv fought to keep every muscle in her body relaxed. As soon as she'd kept one anxious thought at bay, another one broke free inside her mind and caused havoc. There had still been so much more she'd wanted to emotionally unload onto Kam up in their room.

Now, it had to wait for at least a couple more hours.

As they made it over to the van, Dr. Beaumont glanced over to them, then quickly finished up a text message.

One of the side doors slid open.

Kam hopped right in. "G'mornin', Dawn. Although, don't those two words mean the same thing?"

Dawn chuckled as she sent the message off. "I actually haven't heard that one before."

"It's my job as a fledgling writer to be quippy."

Viv climbed in, buckled up, then looked into the back of the mini-van. "How's Phrodo holding up back there?"

Dooo-dooo!

She giggled. "Good morning to you, too, bird-bud."

Once he'd buckled up, Kam glanced through the rear window. "Noticed you've got a trailer hooked up to the back. Is that the distraction?"

Nodding, Dawn pressed the ignition button. "Only if we need it."

The minivan pulled away from the hotel and into traffic.

Unbeknownst to the trio, the man from the previous night had been leaning against the wall a few feet from the hotel's front doors. Putting his newspaper away, he pulled out his cellphone and dialed. "Package is on its way."

Within minutes, they'd parked at the north end of the Lincoln Zoo.

Dawn made a quick exit from the driver's seat and carried on to the van's rear. As the hydraulics let the door open up slowly, she pulled some berries out of a satchel hitched onto her belt. "Here you go, Phrodo."

Viv came up beside the veterinarian and slipped her boyfriend's hoodie on once more. "All right, time to make me look chunky again."

Kam slid the door closed. "It's just feather weight, my dear." He made an audible chuckle. "Maybe that could be our distraction, pretending you're giving birth to a dodo."

The randomness of his idea made Viv burst out laughing. "Kamren… *Ewww.* That has to be the grossest image you've ever put in my mind."

"But it made you laugh."

She went to smack his arm, but patted it instead. "I needed that laugh."

As Phrodo gobbled up the morsels of fruit, Dawn rolled her eyes at the young man's suggestion. "If you two are done joking around, we need to get this bird inside."

"Just trying to lighten the mood," Kam responded with a shrug. He backtracked a step when he noticed the veterinarian's vest swing open for a moment. "Uh, Dr. Beaumont, are you packing?"

Dawn realized he'd seen her gun holster strapped to her body. "It's a *tranquilizer* gun."

When the word 'gun' registered in Viv's ears, she also backed up. "Why does almost everyone we meet have one of those things?"

A sigh left Dawn's mouth. "It's just in case of an emergency."

Inside the building which housed the zoo's hospital, Kamren and Vivienne stepped up to the receptionist's desk. While Viv managed to keep her arms around the hoodie-contained dodo bird, Kam made his face stay deadpan.

The receptionist typed away on her business computer. She finished logging medicinal inventory before looking up at the teenagers. "Good morning, can I help you?"

Kam rubbed a hand against his torso. Tightness seized its first grasp onto his gut. "Hey, uh… We, um…" *Get it together.* "Is there a, um…manager or—"

"Are we able to speak to someone high up here?" More direct, Viv needed things to get moving. *The faster we get through this, the faster we're done with it.* "It's urgent."

Not seeing an animal anywhere near or with them, the pixie-cut receptionist stood up from her rolling desk chair. "Do you need a house call?"

"No, we brought it with us," Viv responded, giving the lady a knowing expression.

A door opened up about ten feet away, and Dr. Isabella Kol marched through with a clipboard in hand. "Krystal, have the antibiotics come in for the aardvark?"

"Should be in later today," Krystal the receptionist answered promptly. "Since you're here, Izzy, these two say they need to speak with someone. Can you help them?"

Dr. Kol gave the teens a dubious glance. "Sorry, I don't really have the time for—"

"You had an animal *escape* yesterday, right?" Kam blurted out, halting the doctor from walking away.

"We did." Dr. Kol kept her response short. "And it's been contained."

"Really?" Kam countered, closing the gap along with Viv. "Because my girlfriend and I stumbled across something that, well, we're pretty sure is supposed to be *extinct.*"

Dr. Kol's cheek and neck muscles twitched.

Viv shifted an arm to hold the creature as she used her other hand to lift up the front of her borrowed hoodie.

It took a moment for Dr. Kol to study the bird. Once the album of bird pictures flipped through her mind, she stepped toward them and held her hand out. "Is that a—"

"A dodo bird, yeah," Kam answered with a nod.

"What did you just say?" The receptionist couldn't see it from her position to confirm the bewildering statement. She'd only taken a few steps away from her desk when Dr. Kol lifted a hand to stop her.

"Krys, hold my calls." Isabella rushed back to the door, then waved the teens on to go through. "Come with me to my office."

THIRTEEN

"SO IS there like, a reward or something for finding the dodo bird?" Kamren stayed close to Vivienne's side as they followed the zoo's doctor. "Being that it's *alive* and all."

Dr. Kol opened her office door and ushered them in. "Why did you think *we* wanted this bird back?"

"Well, it's not that, per se." Viv sat down in one of the chairs. "We found this dodo near our hotel, and figured the best place to take it would be here."

"And the fact that it's a freaking dodo bird..." Kam rested his hands on the top of the plush chair and leaned forward. "...that's a pretty big deal."

Isabella approached the teen girl and held out her hands. "May I see it?"

Viv revealed the dodo bird entirely.

Phrodo turned its head sideways to gawk up at the new human.

Dooo-dooooo.

Dr. Kol chuckled at the creature's greeting call. "Cute little guy."

Half-turning away, Kam pulled out his cellphone and opened his texting app.

We're in. Initiate distraction.

"This one doesn't even look fully grown," Isabella spoke out loud, being careful with her hand placements as she studied the bird. "You said you found it near your hotel?"

"Yeah." Viv did her best to add to the ruse. "It was in some bushes across the street."

Isabella crouched down to pick it up, but the dodo skittered back to Viv's legs. "Oh, I'm sorry. Seems fond of you, though."

Viv leaned over and rubbed her fingers along the back of the bird's head. "Somehow Phrodo and I bonded. He definitely has an inquisitive personality."

"Excuse me, you named it *Phrodo*...the dodo?" Isabella spoke with a bit of a laugh. "That's priceless."

Kam piped up. "I like to think so, and don't forget the P-h." He turned again to hide his tapping fingers on his phone's screen.

Beaumont? Where the heck is the distraction?

Back to standing straight up, Isabella rubbed her hands together. "I'll have to contact my superiors about this." She recalled Drew wanting to show her the dodo bird he'd acquired the day before. Of course, she couldn't let the two kids know about the secret operations. "This is a... *unique* specimen to observe. As you said, it's supposed to be extinct."

With the phone still in his grasp, Kam shoved it and his hand into his pant pocket. "The only explanation we could think of was those rifts going crazy last year."

Dr. Kol had made it around to the front of her desk. "Wait...*you know* about the time rifts?"

Viv chewed on her bottom lip, hoping they wouldn't be giving too much information away about themselves. "Unfortunately."

Kam made his way over to place a hand on his girlfriend's shoulder for a squeeze. "We live close to the Utah SauraCorps museum."

"Really?" Isabella sat down, surprise on her face as she logged into her laptop. "What are you doing way out here then?"

Arms crossed, Viv didn't have to lie. "This little bird-brain interrupted our cross-country vacation."

Once more, Kam whipped out his mobile and nearly fumbled it. Every second he stood in the office, the more his chest tightened. He shot off another text:

ANY DAY NOW!

Dr. Kol opened up her e-mail window. "Well, I appreciate you taking more time out of your vacation to—"
THWACK-CRUNCH!

Wooden door trim splintered into the room.

Isabella jumped as her office door had flown open. "What the—"

Pthew!

Kam and Viv's shocked faces stared at the tranquilizer dart in Dr. Kol's left pectoral. Their collective gazes flew over to the intruder.

Viv leapt out of her chair. "Beaumont?"

Kam waved his phone's screen at the veterinarian. "Is your phone off or—"

"Sorry, kids." Dawn had lowered the gun after incapacitating Dr. Kol. She stared at the floor for a moment, taking a deep breath before looking back up. "This isn't personal."

Pthew-pthew!

FOURTEEN

SALTY AIR wafted into Vivienne's nose as she woke. Blood pounded through her head, which delayed her from opening her eyes. Taking an even deeper breath, she also discerned a metallic odour drifting around her.

Probably just another bad dream.

She lifted her right arm, then let it drape over a sleeping Kamren beside her. "Kam…. Kamren, wake up."

About to turn over, Viv winced due to laying on a hard surface.

The total opposite from their comfy hotel bed.

Kam expelled a large breath before mumbling, "Don't forget…to stay after the credits."

"Kam, you're sleep-talking again." As the throbbing in her head dissipated a bit, Viv finally opened her drowsy eyes. "What?"

Near-complete darkness surrounded her.

Small holes lined the tops of the walls around them,

letting in bits of some light.

She sat up, straining her vision to glance all around. "What…is this?" Viv patted herself down to find she still wore clothes. Extending her hands out to touch what she'd been sleeping on, she swayed her fingers around.

Dusty plywood sat beneath her.

No chair sat in a corner where she'd plopped her purse.

"Yee-ow." Kam lifted his head up, realizing he'd been sleeping on his stomach. "Feels like I slept on a rock."

Groaning as she stood up, Viv brought her hands to the sides of her face. Pieces of jumbled recent memories tried to fit back together. "Kamren, *where* are we?"

"Viv, I don't…." On his feet, Kam staggered a couple of steps away from her. A subtle shifting gave him a slight sense of imbalance. "I don't know." His outstretched hand made contact with a hard, cold material. Running his fingers along the corrugated metal, he racked his brain over what they could be inside of. "It's some kind of…big metal box?"

Tears slipped between Viv's eyes and hands as she grew more frantic. "But *where are we,* Kam?" Everywhere she turned to look, even though her eyes had adjusted, nothing made sense. Her right hand touched a tender spot on her shoulder. *"Agh,* that's—ow, that's tender."

Kam kept heading toward one end of their rectangular confinement. "Are you hurt?"

"My shoulder, it's…." It dawned on her. "Beaumont. She… She *shot* us, didn't she?"

Rolling his own arm up and down in its socket, Kam

experienced the same pain. "The gun." The moment Dawn Beaumont had burst into the office flashed into his mind. "She tranq'd us."

"No." Viv couldn't stop both of her hands from shaking in front of her. An invisible vice choked her and forced air out of her lungs. Every breath she took became harder to keep down. "This can't... This can't be happening *again.*"

Concern pushed Kam back toward her, making him take her flustered hands within his. "Viv, listen to me—"

"We were supposed to be *done* with this frigging dinosaur and time travel world, Kamren." She yanked away from him. Of all the feelings swirling inside of her, animosity and infuriation claimed residence in her voice. "I can't believe *you* dragged us back into it."

"You serious right now?" His chest ached differently, her insult lodging deep beneath the skin. *"You're* the one who saved the dodo." He never thought love and disappointment could be felt at the same time, yet both brawled with each other in his tone. "If you wanted to be done with all that, *you* should've left it at the zoo."

"And leave it to people who would do who knows what with it?" Viv shook her head just as much as her legs vibrated. "We should've left it with Beaumont and *moved on,* Kam. You didn't have to sign us up for Sebastian's damn mission."

"Right, so you're allowed to save an animal but I'm not? That's rich, Viv." He didn't want to get in her face, but the more they threw faults at each other, the closer he came. "And how was I supposed to know *Beaumont* was working for the *bad guys?"*

"We're supposed to be on *our vacation,* Kamren." Her cheeks had become flushed and sopping from tears. "This *clearly* is not that."

Exasperated, he threw his arms up. "And clearly I made a mistake, I'm sor—"

"Why did you agree to this?"

"You want to know *why?*"

"Yes, Kam, *why?*"

"Because I don't want to be what you called me a year ago!" Inadequacy seized his entire being. He couldn't look her in the eye. *"You saved* E-A from the giant millipede while I…."

Numbness overtook Viv, causing her to be silent.

Kam barely croaked out, "I froze."

She failed to find a reply as her mouth hung open.

"Dammit, Viv, can't you see?" Shame covered his face as he glanced into her tear-filled gaze. "I don't want to be frozen over on the sidelines of life anymore." Clearing his throat, the pause enabled him to obtain solidity in his voice. "Sidelines are for people who don't want to make a difference."

As much as she still held some resentment, she took a step closer to him. "But…sidelines allow us to go on road trips and start a life together. Sidelines keep us safe." She reached out, placing a hand on his arm. "Keeps you *with me."*

After wiping his face with his free hand, he mustered a deep breath to the base of his lungs. "I'm *sorry,* Vivienne." He managed a few more glimpses into her turquoise eyes. "If I'd known wanting to save the dinosaurs would've taken us here—"

"Want to know why I keep having nightmares?"

Kam remained quiet but nodded.

Viv sniffled before continuing. "When you didn't make it through the rift with me, I...." She slid her grasp down to sandwich his hand between hers. "And then I realized you'd pushed me through before you could even—"

"Viv, you know I—"

"I thought I'd lost you," she blurted out, pulling his hand up to her heart. "And all these nightmares are of me losing you over and over and over again." Her voice shook as she confronted what she'd wanted to tell him in the hotel room. "And this...."

As her eyes grew accustomed to the dark, she looked all around the ominous metallic container they stood in.

He joined her in gazing around before coming back to her watery stare.

Viv brought her other hand to his cheek. "I *can't* lose you again."

Every emotion churning through Kamren stopped.

Every offense she'd hurled in his direction melted away. Only one thought entered his mind and latched on tight. "Vivienne, I'm sorry for my mistakes, and I know this isn't the perfect moment, but I need to...."

He patted his hand against his pant pocket.

Gone.

The little black box.

Kam opened his eyes wide. *Gone? No, where is—*

Clicks and metallic screeches echoed from the far end of

the chamber.

Viv pressed herself into Kam, who in turn wrapped her up in his arms.

As much as they wanted to know who'd captured them, they also feared the worst.

The large door opened with an obnoxious creak.

Among the few people outside, one man stepped forward.

"If you two are done with your emotional rollercoaster, come with me."

FIFTEEN

OUT IN one of the tempered glass-domed enclosures, Sebastian joined his staff in checking on each animal's well-being. Keeping the dinosaurs and other prehistoric creatures alive and safe gave him a purpose he now cherished.

Since he'd initiated the new version of SauraCorps, he loved getting more hands-on. New enclosures had been built to house rescued time-displaced creatures. With every new arrival, he'd even taken the time to appreciate their individual personality and quirks.

Like Trudy the troodon, he'd also bonded with quite a few of them.

At the moment, he'd been feeding some almost full-grown iguanodons.

With two of their heads up close and personal, Sebastian grinned as one scooped half an apple out of his palm. His other hand rubbed the second iguanodon's crest, as if petting an overgrown, scaley horse. "You've really grown, haven't you, Wilma?" He took his now empty hand and scratched the other dinosaur's chin as it munched on the fruit. "Don't eat that too fast now, Fred. It's like we don't feed you or something."

Wilma the iguanodon closed her eyes and nestled her head into his shoulder. She made a little honk of contentment while getting a head scratch from him.

"You must be ready to lay your clutch soon eh, Wilma? Aiden and Olivia will probably want to take one of your babies home with them." Sebastian smiled and spoke with fondness. His two kids always loved spending time with infant dinosaurs as much as puppies or kittens. As eager as he'd been to see how many eggs Wilma would produce, he heard Felicia in the back of his mind. *"We're exceeding comfortable space for these dinosaurs."*

Over by a golf cart, one of the vet techs heard a phone going off on the seat. "Hey, Seb, your phone!"

"All right." He patted Wilma on the side of her head. "Don't give Fred a hard time, okay?" Sprinting over to the cart, he picked up his phone just before the ringtone finished. "Hello? This is—"

"How's my *old friend* keeping these days?"

Instantly, Sebastian recognized the proper English accent. A torrent of vile thoughts and curses clamored around in his head, but none of them made it to his open mouth.

"Sabretooth got your tongue, Sharpe?"

"For some reason, I don't think you called to catch up, *Blake,*" Sebastian responded, revulsion lacing every word.

A nonchalant chuckle preceded the Englishman's reply. "On the contrary, chap. I'm just as interested in your little prehistoric preserve as you are."

"Not for the same reasons, I'm sure," Sebastian didn't realize how tight he'd been squeezing his phone. "Is there a point to this call, Arrowsmith?"

"Such hostility, and to an old workmate, no less." Blake maintained an unruffled tone. "I'd hoped to extend an invitation to do business togeth—"

"Guess you never got the memo." Sebastian sat down in the golf cart to try and stop his body from vibrating due to animosity. "I don't work like that anymore."

"That's rather disappointing."

"Not for me."

A drawn-out sigh came from Arrowsmith. "Pity. Especially since I was curious to know your thoughts concerning my presentation."

About to make a comeback, puzzlement and unease engulfed Sebastian. *"Presentation?* What are you—"

"Mr. Sharpe!" One of the workers waved their arms

around, then pointed skyward. "What's that?"

A drone of sorts soared overtop of the enclosure.

It hovered for a moment before recalibrating and swaying to the right by a few feet. It began glowing a blueish hue in the underside's center.

Sebastian exited the small electric vehicle, subconsciously taking the cellphone away from his ear. Fixated on the piece of tech, he lowered his gaze to ground level.

An iguanodon slept peacefully.

Directly below the drone.

"Wilmaaaa!"

Sebastian shot away from the cart as fast as his legs could push him. He continued shouting the dinosaur's name to try and make it wake and move.

"Come *on,* Wilm—"

ZEEUU-ZEEUU-ZEEUU-BWOOOOM!

Time rift energy beamed down, then dissipated into nothingness.

Wilma no longer slept on the grass.

Rage built up within Sebastian. He'd hoped control over space-time energy would've never fallen into the wrong hands again. *This is going to mess with everything again.*

Arrowsmith had control.

Running a frantic hand through his hair, Sebastian cursed under his breath before bringing his cellphone back to his ear. *"Blake,* you piece of—"

"Impressive, isn't it?"

Sebastian clenched his free hand into a fist. "How…are you even able to do—"

"Purchased stolen tech on the black market," Blake answered with complete composure as if it were an everyday occurrence. "Someone found it among the rubble of an old spy base or something. Thing is, as you can see, these drones are a one-off."

Gazing back up, Sebastian noted the fritzed-out device. "And...?"

Arrowsmith let out a single chuckle. "Care to do business together?"

"I already told you, I'm *not*—"

"And I'm sending you a picture..." Arrowsmith paused to tap the screen of his phone. "...of *two reasons* for you to agree."

Ding!

Sebastian clicked on the received e-mail.

When he opened the image file, his heart sank.

The day before, Dr. Beaumont had texted him to report how everything had gone according to plan at the zoo.

Insurmountable guilt assaulted his mind and threatened to strangle his entire body.

Kamren and Vivienne sat in chairs with ropes tied around their abdomens.

Their hands were bound by zip ties.

It had only been a year ago that Sebastian had committed to banishing the teenagers to a prehistoric world. He'd done what he thought he had to do to further his purpose. Now a changed man, he stared at the photo with dread in his eyes. *I can't let them go through that again.*

From the phone's speakers, Arrowsmith spoke up. "I'll

call you back in an hour. Should give you enough time to gather what you need."

"If you hurt them…." Sebastian grit his teeth together. "…I will call in every favor owed to me to take you down."

"Chat later, *friend.*"

Once Arrowsmith had concluded the call, Sebastian let his hand fall to the side. The man he'd been struggling to track down and put a stop to had just made a grand move.

One that couldn't be ignored.

In an emotional daze, Sebastian called up the only person he could think of. "Felicia, I need you to get my luggage bags out of storage."

"You're leaving?"

"Yeah, listen…" An anxious hand rubbed the back of his neck. "…I *have to save* Kam and Viv."

SIXTEEN

"NOW THAT'S taken care of, it's time to figure out what to do with the two of you." Blake Arrowsmith slipped his phone into the breast pocket of his grey, double-breasted overcoat. "I must say, having you stumble into my operations has turned out to be quite a blessing in disguise."

Kamren glared at him, gauging whether to make a deflective wisecrack or not.

Though Vivienne had been tied to the chair beside him, nothing could harness the intense spinning of negative thoughts in her mind.

"You're allowed to speak, you know." Arrowsmith placed himself a few feet away from them. "After that display in the shipping container, I'm surprised you're—"

"So *you're* the fecal sludge of a human being who's dealing dinosaurs," Kam finally blurted out. Once he realized what his brain had made him say, every muscle in his body locked up.

"Bravo, boy." An unimpressed expression washed onto Arrowsmith's face. "And your attempt at an insult insults me."

"Don't encourage him," Viv spit out, hating the man in front of her while disappointed by her constrained boyfriend's snark.

Kam had been trying to wriggle his bound hands for the past twenty minutes. He'd finally given up. "Why is it that so many villains are British? The only good thing you've given the world is fish and chips and Earl Grey tea."

Arrowsmith grinned. "Not a football fan?"

"Only if the *soccer* ball is being kicked straight at your face—"

"Kamren." Viv sent an icy stare his way. "This guy could literally *kill us.*"

Two snaps of the Englishman's fingers signaled his guard in the room. "Which reminds me. Eccleston, untie them."

The sudden change perplexed the teenagers.

"Thing is, simply being here means you've already seen too much." Nonchalance blended with superiority as it took over Arrowsmith's expression and tone. "I'll still dangle you in front of Sebastian for what I need, then you'll be disposed of." He gave them an indifferent look as if to say 'it's just business'.

Kam and Viv exchanged terrified glances.

One word had stuck out to them.

Disposed.

"By tomorrow morning, we'll arrive at our destination." Arrowsmith marched over to the door and opened it. "For now, this storage room will be outfitted into your living quarters, and should you require any supervision, Miss Beaumont is now your detail."

As she strolled into the room, Dawn met the teen's glares of absolute contempt. "Good morn—"

"Is it?" Kam crossed his arms. "And clearly, you're not a *veterinarian.*"

Dawn still wore her vet satchel. "I am, actually—"

"One that *shoots* people, then?" Viv rubbed her sore area once more. "Weren't you supposed to be working for Sebastian?"

Arrowsmith flashed a devious grin as he rubbed Dawn's back. "Sharpe should really get to know who his true friends are."

"Ah, I get it now." Kam made sure his eyes had locked onto Beaumont's. "You're a backstabbing, people-shooting veterinarian."

Her eyes pierced right back into his. "And now that I'm your warden of sorts, I'd be *careful* what *you say to me* from now on."

Hearing those rigid, chilling words, Viv rubbed her arms up and down. They still had no idea of where they were in the world. Getting on the bad side of people who could hurt them, or worse, took supremacy as the last thing she wanted. *How* are *we going to get out of this alive?* She cleared unease from her throat. "We *won't* cause any trouble." She swung her gaze over to her boyfriend. *"Right,* Kamren?"

He studied the faces of their captors before looking into Viv's terrified eyes. They'd just had their first fight. Doing the right thing would hopefully help keep her anxiety manageable. *Be brave, just don't be an idiot.* Once a calm breath had traveled through his lungs, he nodded. "No trouble. I promise."

"Excellent," Arrowsmith exhaled with the least bit of interest, checking his watch. "Now that's settled, I'm off to tend to other business."

"See you later, hon." Dawn leaned over, receiving a kiss from him.

Judgment overtook Kam's face. "Someone get me a bucket, I might hurl—*ow!*"

Viv elbowed him in the side. "*Seriously,* Kam. Keep it together."

"Might have to get a bucket in here, anyway," Dawn mentioned while scanning the room for general sizing of items. "Unless you've already found your sea legs."

About to comment on the bucket and their toilet situation, Kam backed up a step. "Wait, did you just say—"

"*Sea* legs?" An already buzzing Viv received a new wave of unease. "As in *ocean?*"

"Right." Beaumont opened the door with an expectant expression. "You two missed quite a bit. Come along."

The reluctant pair didn't say a word as they followed the woman down a reinforced and unfamiliar hallway. Details of access points and furnishings reminded them of things they'd seen in certain movies.

Faint echoes of a guttural noise barely touched Viv's ears. "Hear that?"

Kam tried to hone in on it. "Something…groaning?"

At the top of a set of metal-grated stairs, Dawn opened a

heavy door to the right.

Sunlight poured through, accompanied by the clamoring of seagulls.

Vivienne stepped out first, followed by a flabbergasted Kamren.

The salty air they'd inhaled earlier finally made sense.

Dr. Beaumont passed them and placed her hands on the railing. "Welcome to the North Atlantic Ocean."

"North…Atlantic…*Ocean?*"Vivienne staggered forward, letting her hands clasp onto the shipping boat's sturdy top rail. The sheer lack of land among the vastness of blue seawater gave her a different kind of seasickness.

"Hold up, how much time did we lose?" Kamren turned to address the dinosaur veterinarian for a clearer explanation. "When were we taken from Chicago?"

Beaumont hadn't been a huge fan of him from the day they met, but she accepted his current confusion to be rightly justified. "We kept you safely sedated during the thirty-six-hour trip—"

"Safely?" Sarcasm coated Kam's tone. "Thank you *soooo much* for thinking of our safety, *friend.*"

"Thirty…." Kam's voice dropped off as he sifted his fingers through his hair. "*Thirty-six* hours?"

Taking a moment to reign in a heated reply, Dawn took in a breath of fresh, salty air. "I understand you're disoriented, but—"

"Yeah, *no freaking crap* we're disoriented." Viv spun around to begin a verbal assault. Her earlier fight with Kam had primed her. "You pretended to work for Sebastian, shot us, kidnapped us, and put us on a-a-a massive boat with the Godfather of dino-traffickers who's willing to off us at any moment!" Spit had flown from her mouth as she laser-beamed her gaze into Dr. Beaumont. "I can't… I can't do this."

Hoping to give some comfort, Kam reached out and slipped his hand onto her wrist.

Viv yanked her hand away. "No, Kam, I just…. Not right now."

Once she'd stuffed her hands in her pant pockets, Viv left to walk off the anxious energy building up inside of her. She didn't even look behind or take in the ocean view. A hurricane of negative thoughts pummelled her mind. *Why do our lives keep getting turned upside down? Why us?* About a hundred feet away from the others, she let her body lean onto the railing to linger on the thought: *Will we live through this?*

Kam still stood near the veterinarian. He wanted to chase after his girlfriend, but something told him to give her some space. *I need her to be okay.* His chest tightened. *I'll do everything it takes to keep her okay.*

Dawn gazed down the walkway to the teen girl, then looked back at Kam.

Then she took a quick glance in the opposite direction.

"Listen, Kam, I don't have—"

A generic cellphone ringer went off.

Dawn's upper lip twitched as she pulled out her phone and placed it to her ear. "What's up?"

"Asset number eight-zero-three is in labor," one of

Arrowsmith's men reported.

"What? I thought she wasn't due for another—"

"It's happening *now.*"

Dawn hung up and placed a hand on Kam's shoulder, who pulled away. "Listen, you and Viv need to come with me."

Kam noticed the haste in her voice. "Does it concern us?"

"If you don't come with me, it will."

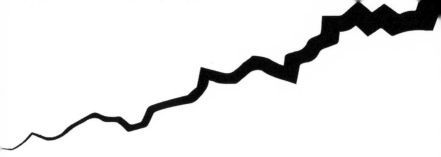

SEVENTEEN

DOWN A level, Dr. Beaumont had led the teenagers to a large open area within the carrier ship. A few of Arrowsmith's employees tended to their duties, including three of them on the opposite side by a large hairy mass.

When Kamren stepped through the double doors, he noticed the multiple dinosaurs and prehistoric animals peering back at them through their cages and cramped enclosures.

The stench of moist metal and barnyard pinpointed Vivienne's nose. "Oh God, this place wreaks like—"

KREEEEAAAAW!

Clang!

Throwing herself backward into Kam, Viv stared back at a frighteningly familiar dinosaur. "That's a ther... Therizin...."

Wha-bang!

One of the saber-like claws slipped between the metal bars as the others clashed within. The agitated therizinosaurus cried out, glaring down at the teenagers.

"Those nightmares will be back now." Viv pushed Kam away from the creature. "That's the one that chased after me."

"Dear Lord, that would be terrifying." Kam's eyes had opened wide. "You never told me it was the *Wolverine* of dinosaurs."

Meanwhile, Dawn proceeded to instruct the others on how to deal with the pregnant creature. "Everyone, we'll need to let her out into the open for this."

"You out of your mind?" one of Arrowsmith's men countered.

"She needs to sway and move her hind legs around to help push the baby out," Dr. Beaumont fired back as birthing procedures and possible issues flipped through her mind. "Let her out now, or we might lose her *and* the calf."

As the three employees gave each other wary looks, they knew losing the mother meant less of a paycheck. One of them opened the large gate which led to the open floor in the middle of the ship. The other two remained close with electric prodding poles in hand.

The teens came up behind the veterinarian.

Similar to when Kam had been thrust into the primeval past and came across dinosaurs for the first time, he gazed in amazement. "That's a woolly mammoth, isn't it?"

"Surprised you didn't call it a Snuffleupagus," Viv quipped.

"Close, it's an imperial mammoth, and she might get a little vigorous, so stay back a bit, kids." Dawn put herself between the fifteen-ton animal and them, keeping her hands up in defense.

♀ mammoth

4.5m

5m

Every step the mammoth took out of its enclosure shook the floor. It parted its back legs as far as they could go, and gave a decent push.

"Give her some space," Dawn called out, noticing one of the men closing in. "Keep an eye on her tusks, those will break bones."

The mammoth's deep trumpeting rumbled through the area as it managed to work through some contractions. Its thunderous steps helped to reposition her enormous body. Woolly strands trembled as it planted itself once more and engaged its muscles for another push.

"Come on, girl." As much as Beaumont's love for animals made her want to get closer, her respect for its size and unpredictability kept her at a safe distance. "That's it, momma, keep it up."

The awe on Kam's face quickly turned to nausea. "That's…

um...." Once he caught sight of the embryotic sac's slimy beginnings, he immediately turned around. "I don't think I need to see this."

As for Viv, witnessing a prehistoric life being born in the present took away her anxiety for the moment. The mammoth's primal bellows of pain mixed with the wondrous, natural experience of a creature coming into existence became something beautiful to her.

Brushing a hand up and down the mammoth's front leg, Dawn took a chance and placed the other hand on the tusk to maneuver with the animal's movements. "I know it hurts, but you're doing great, missy."

Viv winced as the mother emitted another agonizing cry along with another push.

"And it's *almoooost...theeeere....*" Dawn hollered, crouching to get an even better look at the calf's progress.

BA-DUM!

With its trunk waving in the air, the enormous woolly mammoth's wail of relief made the entire room vibrate.

"Is it out?" Hands on his knees, Kam didn't look over. "Is the baby out?"

Viv snorted at her boyfriend. "Remind me to never have kids with you."

One of Arrowsmith's men stared at the lifeless lump on the floor. "It's...*not moving.*"

"Should we help it?" asked another.

The mother mammoth turned to gain a better vantage point of her newborn.

"It might have some liquid in its lungs." Beaumont kept

her guard up toward the adult as she backed away from its head. Then she noticed one of the men heading toward the infant out of the corner of her eye. "Don't touch it!"

The sudden outburst made Kam finally take a look.

RRRRAAAAAAHHHH!

Alarmed, the mammoth charged forward and pulled one of its giant feet back.

Crunch!

The foot connected with the side of the man, sending him flying into hard cage bars.

One of the other men fired up his electric prod.

"Stop!" Dawn waved her arms up and down. "She's trying to save her baby!"

The guy raised his voice. "Then why did it kick him?"

"It tried to kick the *infant,* he got *in the way.*" Dawn shook her head, once again reminded to never get in the way of nature. "That's how they get their baby's lungs working."

Even more frantic than before, the mother swung her head side to side. Its right tusk whooshed past one of the employee's heads before swinging back, taking their legs out from under them.

Viv took Kam's hand as she started to put distance between them and the raging mammoth.

When he felt her hand in his, he squeezed it.

Dawn pointed to their exit. "Guys, head back through the doors we came through."

As she'd finished her sentence, the lumbering pachyderm turned its attention to them.

All three of them sprinted toward the doors.

Viv pushed Kam through the doors first, then held it open for Dr. Beaumont as she barrelled through.

Smash!

One of the thick tusk ends knocked a door right off its hinges. Pulling its head back, the mammoth retreated into the open area.

"Are you guys…okay?" Dawn asked the teens between heavy breaths. "Good God."

"I think so." Viv checked herself over, thankful she hadn't been bashed by the battered door, or the mammoth's tusk for that matter.

After catching her breath, Dawn inched closer to the damaged doors. Through the opening, she watched as the mother mammoth rushed over to her newborn.

It struck the baby in the underbelly with its foot.

No signs of life could be seen or heard.

Staring out the window of the intact door, Viv found herself rooting for the little creature. It gave her something hopeful among all the craziness she'd been pulled into.

With an alarming wail, the mammoth swung its foot again, then brought its eye down to check on her calf. Its left tusk nudged the baby before intertwining their trunks together.

"Come on," Viv whispered to herself. "Come on, little guy."

Lifting the baby's head up for airflow, the mother spun it around.

A gasp came from the infant.

Bringing its eye closer, the adult mammoth noted the mouth movements. Air finally entered its calf's lungs.

"It's alive," Dawn announced, entering the room as she figured the mammoths would be focused on each other. "Hopefully momma won't be so anxious and can let us help her."

For the first time since she'd woken up on the ship, Viv wore a big grin. "I've always wanted to meet a baby elephant. Do you think...we could maybe pet it?"

"Let's give them time to get acquainted with each other first." Dr. Beaumont kept her footsteps silent to keep the new mammoth family relaxed.

"I will say one thing," Kam placed a hand on his chest. "I'll never *forget* this."

EIGHTEEN

FELICIA STOOD in the bedroom doorway. "So the elusive Blake Arrowsmith just called you out of the blue?"

"Yup." Due to Blake's vague instruction of 'gather what you need', Sebastian tucked a pair of pants beside a dress shirt in his luggage bag, then put his worrisome thoughts off to the side for a moment. "With an encrypted number, too."

She crossed an arm and put a fist up to her mouth. "I can't believe he's got those poor teens. They've been through enough."

"Which is why I need to do this," he responded with resolve. Though he'd eventually come to terms with the ordeal from a year ago, he hadn't truly forgiven himself for changing the lives of the two teenagers. "Blake is a desperate man, and if I don't give him what he wants…."

Felicia narrowed her gaze at him. "Why is it you seem to know exactly what he wants, but I don't even have an inkling?"

He rubbed his teeth over his bottom lip.

She read the reserved look on his face. "Seb, what aren't you telling me?"

Leaving the bag unzipped, he rotated to perch on the bed. *Never thought in a million years this would come back to haunt me.* He sucked in a deep breath. "SauraCorps…had *deeper secrets* than the rift."

For a moment, Felicia lost all sense of replying as she glanced around the room. "Mind revealing that now?"

Sebastian closed his eyes, despising his past decisions. "Other than taking most of my earnings to pay for lawyer fees to see my kids, I also paid some of our scientists under the table for…a little side project."

"You had…." She placed one of her palms against her forehead as her other hand went to her hip. "Of course you had off-book operations. *That explains* the missing numbers in your bank accounts back then."

"And we—wait, *what?*" His baffled stare connected with her harsh glare. "You'd been viewing my accounts?"

She shrugged. "Guess you're not the only one with extra secrets."

The upsetting information sunk in as he returned to divulging. "Back then, I viewed rift energy as something we could try to control in a bigger way. It had more potential than being a simple doorway." Sebastian wrung his hands together and cracked some knuckles as he gazed out the bedroom window to the dinosaur enclosure. "Blake marched into my office one night when I'd been putting in late hours. He saw the plans on my desk and wouldn't leave until I told him everything."

Felicia rubbed her tongue along the inside of her cheek as she absorbed his every word. "So that's why you two stopped getting along."

"I only wanted to use the space-time energy to make SauraCorps—well, *mostly me*—more efficient at collecting prehistoric creatures," he continued, his tone saturated in regret. "But what Blake wanted…. I told him what he wanted to use it for would have *catastrophic* repercussions."

Catching on to his train of thought, she began nodding. "And what he wants from you could help him."

"He's already completed phase one." Sebastian pointed an open hand to the window, still able to view the fritzed drone on top of the glass dome. "That thing just *teleported* Wilma to… Only Blake knows where."

Felicia's eyes flared open in realization. "And once you trade your information for the kids?"

Standing back up, Sebastian gazed out over his revamped SauraCorps endeavor. "If you thought haphazard rifts were scary, this could destroy everything even quicker."

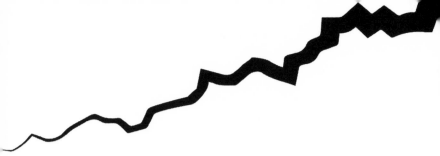

NINETEEN

"MILLIE." KAMREN stayed close to his girlfriend in the creature storage room. "Decent name for a woolly mammoth, don't you think?"

"There he goes again," Vivienne remarked, scratching the baby pachyderm behind its ear.

Once the mother had calmed down and the adrenaline from giving birth had subsided, it had laid down to rest right outside of its enclosure.

After Dawn had run some tests on the calf, she'd given the okay for the others to approach and interact with it as long as the mother didn't protest.

"The baby should be named Walter." Kam brought his eyes down to the animal's inquisitive, big eye. "Or Winston, or maybe—"

"I'm naming it Downey," Viv mentioned with finality in her voice. "Because it's soft like downy, but with the e-y so it's not so on the nose."

Kam snorted. "No relation to Robert?"

"Back to Marvel references, huh?"

"Definitely picturing a mammoth with an Iron Man suit." Amused, Kam chuckled as the mammoth's little trunk wrapped around his arm.

"If you're all done playing around…." Blake Arrowsmith strolled past the mangled door unfazed. "Holsinger, get a tag on its ear." Cellphone in hand, he tapped on the screen a few times. "The infant should get us about five to ten million, I'm guessing."

Still petting Downey the mammoth calf, Viv glared at the Englishman. "It isn't even an hour old and you're already putting a *price tag* on it?"

Blake didn't look up from his phone. "Is it male or female?"

Dr. Beaumont answered, "It's a boy."

"Closer to fifteen million then, excellent." Blake continued clicking the touchscreen buttons, updating his list and calculations. When he looked up from the device, he gave no attention to the teenagers. "Coleman, make sure we get an enclosure ready for another arrival in about two minutes."

Kam squinted at the employees as they followed orders. "Arrival? We're in the middle of the ocean."

"On a twisted Noah's ark for dinosaurs," Viv added, getting more irritated by the ship's owner. "Only it's run by the devil."

Blake flicked a corner of his mouth up into a roguish smirk. "Can anyone see if our dinosaur muzzles work on teenagers?"

Kam wore an 'oh my God' face. "Firstly, your jokes are horrible." Then he looked over at Dawn. "Secondly, you're seriously into this twit?"

The veterinarian stared back at him without flinching. "Kamren, go take a walk."

"Is…that your best comeback—"

"Take a walk, *now.*"

Once her 'don't mess with me' tone hit the bulls-eye of his eardrums, he avoided her glare and turned to his girlfriend. "Coming with me?"

She remained crouched beside Downey. "I'm gonna stay."

Disappointed, he took a step closer. "Viv, maybe we should—"

"In case you forgot, we're in a stressful situation and there are no cats for me to pet," she countered with a slight tremor in her voice. "So I'm going to *stay* and *pet* this *fuzzy* mammoth until I'm good."

Kam gave her a longing, wounded stare before turning around.

Wandering away from Viv, he truly understood a new sense of loneliness.

As he strolled along, the first cage to his right housed a young quetzalcoatlus. Noticing the familiar details of its appearance, he placed his hands on the bars and leaned in. "Hey, little guy. Any relation to a Quinley—"

REEAAOOW! REEAAOOW! REEAAOOW!

The adolescent pterosaur jumped forward, racking its beak against the bars as it screeched.

"Jeez, friggin' heck, man!" Kam stumbled backward,

bumping into a smaller structure. He got his breathing under control as he noticed the shoulder-height wooden crate.

Dooo-dooo!

"Phrodo?" Kam lowered himself to get a better view. "That you, birdie?"

A pitter-patter preceded a recognizable feathered face. *Dooo-dooo-dooo.*

"Nice to find a friend in here," Kam remarked as he sat down beside the captive dodo bird. Reaching his right hand into the cage to pat Phrodo's head, he sighed. "It sucks, though. The only person I want to talk to kinda hates me right now."

Phrodo's beak protruded from between the wooden slats and rubbed against Kam's shoulder. *Dooo-dooo.*

"I mean, I get why she's mad at me." Kam continued, sifting his free hand into his coarse dark hair. "But did I know we'd get shot and brought to a freaking boat? No."

Dooo-dooo.

"And I wish she would've told me about her stress and nightmares." His voice radiated devotion and concern as he turned his gaze to the rubber-matted floor. "Now that I look back, I should've noticed it."

Phrodo cocked its head side to side, peering out at the gloomy teen.

"Makes me feel like a *horrible, insensitive* boyfriend."

Dooo-dooo-dooo.

"Thanks, buddy."

Dooo-dooo.

Kam let out a small laugh. "And…I'm having a heart-to-heart with a dodo. Awesome."

An obnoxious alarm echoed through the cargo area.

"Heads up and clear the area!" one of Arrowsmith's workers called out.

Behind the infant mammoth, Dawn shooed it toward its mother while addressing Viv. "You'll have to resume petting your emotional support animal later."

More employees of Arrowsmith's organization formed a perimeter around a central area. Some held heavy-duty rifles while others prepared electrical prods.

The commotion pulled Kam away from Phrodo for the moment. Coming to his girlfriend's side, he slid his hand under her wrist in the hopes of a small form of reconciliation.

When his fingers met Viv's skin, she looked up into his remorse-filled face.

Kam closed his eyes, wishing they were back home.

Her fingers weaved into his.

Opening his eyes, he gave way to a small smile.

"We'll talk later, okay?" Viv rubbed her thumb along his skin.

Unsure of how to respond, he simply picked up her hand and kissed the back of it. "I'd like tha—"

"Asset arrival in twelve…eleven…"

As the man counted down, Kam and Viv kept their eyes on the center of the circling employees.

"Eight…seven…"

The teens gazed up when recognizable crackling emitted

from a glowing blueish light in the ceiling.

"Four...*three...two...one!*"

ZEEUU-ZEEUU-ZEEUU-BWOOOOM!

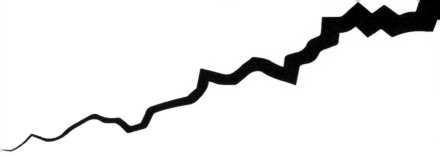

TWENTY

SPACE-TIME ENERGY coursed downward, pulling a large reptilian being from another location to the boat's inner chamber.

Molecule by molecule, large clawed feet led to lean and muscular legs. Once the ethereal, bright blueish beam dissipated, it finished with the dinosaur's sizeable head, which contained rows of steak knife-like teeth.

ROOOOOOOOAAAAAAAAR!

Panic seized Arrowsmith's body and face. "Wasn't it supposed to be asleep in a cage?"

One of his men aimed for the startled dinosaur's neck. "Tómasson's guys said it was!"

Hostility in its eyes, the thirty-foot-long megalosaurus swayed its head back and forth, taking in the armed welcoming party.

Meanwhile, Kamren and Vivienne finally realized how Arrowsmith ran his operations.

♀ megalosaurus

3m

9m

"That was rift energy, wasn't it?" Viv remarked, already stepping back.

"Sure looked like it." Kam noticed her squeezing his hand tighter. "But that was more 'beam me up, rexy.'"

Dawn grabbed Viv's other arm. "And that megalosaurus isn't happy, we should probably leave."

On the other side of the employee barrier from the aggravated therapod, Blake also started for one of the exits. "Tranq it!" As he neared a door, he whipped out his cellphone. "Bloody Kristjan, that's the *last time* we do business."

Heading the opposite way, Dawn led the teenagers past detained prehistoric creatures. "They'll be fine back there, they've handled worse."

Viv kept up with the veterinarian. "Worse than that?"

"Considering the circumstances, I wish that dino would handle them." Kam slowed down as he neared Phrodo's cage. "See who it is, babe?"

Recognizing the dodo excited Viv—the fact that it could excite her also surprised her. "Phrodo!"

Dooo-dooo!

"Why would they lock up a dodo bird?" Viv placed her hand under the padlock. "It's not nearly as vicious as that big thing down there."

Kam opened his mouth to say something, when he looked over at Dr. Beaumont.

A few cages down, Dawn had stuck her arm through one to pet the crest of an iguanodon. "Aw, Wilma, it's going to be okay, girl."

"Got a key to this thing, Doc?" Kam raised his voice while squinting at her. "Viv needs something else to pet."

Dawn pulled her hand out from between the bars. "I do, but I can't just release—"

"Listen, Dawn of the dinosaurs," Kam snapped back, adamancy all over his face. "I've been her boyfriend for about a year now. And let me tell you, you *do not* want Viv on your bad side. Believe me, it's constant sarcasm and scowls." He looked back at Viv, who'd been giving him the expression he'd just described. "See what I mean?"

"Aaaaaauuuuugh!" one of the employees screamed out from behind them. "It's got *my leg!*"

Viv gave Dawn an expectant stare. "Give me the damn dodo. Preferably before that mega-dino comes our way."

On their way back to the holding room, Kam and Viv

walked side by side.

Arrowsmith employees strolled past, giving them peculiar glances.

As Viv avoided meeting their gazes, she found some solace in Phrodo pitter-pattering beside her. The little bird's cute factor helped to keep her mind anchored among the stress of being on the daunting boat.

Since they'd left the dinosaur containment room, Kam had been speculating over what they'd witnessed. "So it isn't exactly a rift, but Arrowsmith has some sort of control over the space-time energy?"

"It's like it came out of nowhere," Viv remarked, then looked down at the dodo bird. "Are they pulling creatures out of the past that way now?"

Kam squinted his left eye while raising his right eyebrow. "It's gone from Stargate to Star Trek. What's next? Splicing rift energy into someone's DNA?"

Viv gave his shoulder a backhanded tap. "That big battle in Washington a few years ago, wasn't the one superhero able to teleport?"

Dr. Beaumont perused e-mails and messages on her phone as she tagged along behind them. She sent off a message before piping up. "They aren't pulling animals from the past."

Halting mid-step, Kam turned to address her. "Care to elaborate?"

Dawn put her phone away as her stomach growled. "How about we have a little chat in the dinette?"

Viv looked over her clothing. "Guess there's no chance

of changing. Gotta love wearing the same outfit two days in a row."

"Going on three days," Kam pointed out. "Half a day in Chicago, Dawn said we were unconscious for a travel day, and we woke up today."

Viv flicked her hand up. "Thanks for the reminder."

Out of all the times he'd heard her using sarcasm, this instance made him wince the hardest. He hung back giving her some space. *If only she knew what I wanted to ask her.* A surge of determination made a plan pop into his head.

Letting the area between him and his girlfriend grow even more, he lowered his voice and matched Dr. Beaumont's pace. "Hey, um… Dawn? Did anyone happen to grab our luggage from the hotel?"

Dawn cleared her throat. "To make it look like you two were never there, I believe they did."

"Would they be on board?"

"I'm pretty sure they—"

"I need mine," Kam whispered, infusing his plea with passion. "Before all of this…" He twirled his index finger around at the general boat. "…I'd been planning on *proposing* to her."

The word made Dawn stiffen.

"I left the ring in my suit jacket." He flexed his cheek muscles, eager to get the pricy piece of jewelry back in his possession. "If Viv and I aren't going to make it, can you at least get that to me?"

Dawn didn't look at the teen as she marched on. "I'll see what I can do."

TWENTY-ONE

NEW YORK

"WE NEED those *eggs!"*

Frantic, the hefty chef left the kitchen through the back. He met with a disheveled café employee outside of a locked door and raised his Bronx-accented voice. "I can't get my patrons omelets if I don't have any eggs."

The younger lady tied the back of her apron. "Sorry I'm late, Dougie. My boyfriend broke up with me this mornin' and it took forever to hail a taxi—"

"Boo-hoo." Dougie pretended to rub his eyes with closed fists. "That's the sixth guy for ya in two months. I don't care if ya had ta run in those little heels, one more late day and you're fired. Ya hear me, Ricki?"

She huffed. "You can't do that, I bring in the most tips."

"Gimme more lip and you won't get any more tips, missy."

"Okay, just…." Ricki huffed while clicking the door's six-digit code. "Let's see how the girls are doin', a'right?"

"*Today* would be great."

Loud clicks and a beep signified the door had unlocked.

Rushing inside, they began checking the baskets.

Dougie ran a hand over his thinning hair. "Three eggs? *Three…eggs?*"

Meanwhile, Ricki had opened a gate to enter a holding pen.

Four pachycephalosauruses stood barred in place with barely any room to move.

♀ PachyCePhalosauRus

1.8 m

4.5 m

HHAAAAWWOOOOOONK!

As soon as one of them began bellowing, the other three joined into an irritable chorus. One of them bashed its domed skull against the metal bars to the left and right.

"Make sure they get their chow," Dougie tried to shout over the dinosaurs as he started scooping the eggs into a carrying basket. "I gotta get back to—"

"They barely ate yesterday's food," Ricki countered,

kicking at the lettuce heads and collard greens in the troughs. "They must be super stressed out or—"

"Then shove it down their throats or somethin'. I don't care what you gotta do to get them to lay," Dougie barked back while returning to the door. "People are starvin' out here."

"Absolutely not." Ricki became incensed at the mere thought of treating the prehistoric creatures as suggested. "I will *not* be party to inhumane—"

"You're fired."

All of the dinosaur racket seemed to diminish as Ricki stared at her ex-boss. The job she'd needed to keep making it month to month vanished.

"Turn your apron in before ya leave," Dougie called over.

Clang!

The metal door closed.

An unemployed Ricki stood alone with the pachycephalosauruses.

"He can't…." As she put the bottom of her palm to her forehead, she set the other hand down on a metal bar. "That's just…."

Scaley hide touched the side of her hand.

The pachycephalosaurus nudged its nose against her fingers while whimpering.

Ricki slid her hand under its chin to rub and scratch it. "He wants me ta leave, huh?"

"Order numba twelve, Krissy!" Dougie rang the bell to notify another waitress.

"Jeez Louise, why's it so breezy in here?" one of the other cooks remarked. "Did you turn the A/C on or—"

"I didn't touch nothin'," Dougie retorted as he returned to the main cooking station.

"Which technically means you did touch somethin'."

"Don't get smart, Chad." Exasperated, Dougie waved his spatula around. "How 'bout you go check, I'm behind here."

Chad left his chopping post and turned a corner of the island kitchen layout.

The righthand back door had been left open.

"Who the heck left this—"

HWOOOOOOOOOONK!

Nine hundred pounds of dinosaur barreled through.

The pachycephalosaurus' ten-inch-thick, boney skull connected with Chad's upper body.

Airborne, the lanky cook flailed his arms as he hollered in pain.

As he landed in a double sink, his dazed eyes witnessed the other three fifteen-foot-long creatures entering the kitchen. "Good Lord."

One of the angered dinosaurs dragged its left foot back, scuffing up the linoleum floor.

It lowered its head and snorted.

"Dougie!" Chad screamed out. "They're out!"

The head chef whipped a towel over his shoulder as he came around. "What do ya mean they're—"

THWACK-CRUNCH!

Propelled by the dinosaur's destructive skull, Dougie flew past the kitchen, over the bar-top and crash-landed into a table.

Patrons within the café cried out in confusion and horror.

Outside, Ricki tossed her stained apron in a sidewalk garbage bin. "Be free, ladies."

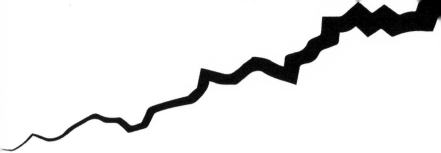

TWENTY-TWO

"WAIT, YOU mean this food is *free?"* Vivienne's eyes opened wide as she scanned through a tablet. The list of available dishes sounded uber-expensive. Once food aromas in the ship's dinette had entered her nostrils, she fully realized how hungry she'd become.

"Blake takes care of his people," Dawn mentioned, already pressing buttons on a second handheld screen.

Though Kamren needed Dr. Beaumont to come through for him, he made a small scowl. "Arrowsmith's really got you *'Jaded',* huh?"

Viv paused her menu scan to roll her eyes. "Another *Aerosmith* pun?"

"Thanks for making me feel old." Dawn tsked while leaning back in her chair. "And think what you will, you've only seen one side of him."

Both teens looked at her with skepticism.

"You mean the dinosaur trafficker side?" Viv rebutted,

then looked down to Phrodo, who napped by her feet. "Who also treats the creatures like they're not worth as much as he sells them for—"

"Don't forget he threatens teenagers," Kam snuck in.

"That too," Viv carried on without missing a beat. "That's the side you're referring to, right? Or are we mistaken?"

Rather than bicker with them, Dawn kept silent.

"Oh, and look at this," Kam noticed a second tab to the ship's menu. "Dishes made with dinosaurs?"

"Are you kidding me?" Viv's hunger fed her infuriation as Kam pressed his finger to the tablet. "Juvenile brachiosaurus shank? Triceratops au jus?"

"They've got fried Compy legs with a blue cheese dip," Kam added before a disgusted grimace took over him. "That's... I can't even...."

Viv looked to where he'd been pointing. "Elderberry *nundasuchus* tenderloin with kale stem pesto?"

"There goes my appetite." Kam left the table and began pacing as he weaved his arms together tight against his chest.

Dawn hadn't expected the boy's reaction. "What's up with—"

"He *befriended* a nundasuchus after we were thrown through the rift." Viv set the tablet down to examine her offended boyfriend staring off into the distance. This had been the first time she'd ever seen him truly disturbed. "He named it Nandy."

Tension flickered throughout Dawn's face. "I see—"

Whump!

Kam slammed his open palms onto the tabletop. "How do I know that isn't the *actual Nandy* on the menu, huh?"

Dawn didn't look at him while raising a non-confrontational hand. "Like I said earlier, Blake isn't pulling dinosaurs from—"

"Don't veterinarians have a *code of ethics* they follow?" Kam spit back at her.

Among everything he'd said to her since they'd met, Dawn sensed outrage being sparked within her chest. "You don't want to get into an ethics discussion with me, kid."

Viv pointed a hand at the woman. "Kamren, she *helped* a mammoth give birth, then *looked after* the baby."

Kam shook his head. "Because she's paid with *dinosaur blood money* to do it."

Clang!

Dawn kicked her chair back.

Ka-thwump!

With a hold on Kam's arm, the veterinarian pinned him face down to the top of the table.

Phrodo woke up with a screech and flittered its wings in distress.

"Jeez." It took Viv a moment to keep up with the swift event. "Dawn, let him go."

Cheek to table, Kam tried to wriggle free. "Get off, Dr. Do-wrong—"

"Listen, *Kamren,* you can think of me however you want," Dr. Beaumont stated, putting more of her bodyweight onto him. "But you don't even have *an inkling* of what I've *been through,* and what I've *sacrificed* for…."

About to reply, Viv caught the few droplets trickling from Dawn's eyes.

One of the tears landed in front of Kam's face.

As more drops of salty moisture hit the table, the three of them said nothing.

Dawn released her grip on the teen.

Slowly, Kam stood back up and glanced between his girlfriend and the troubled woman. "I…um… I'm sorry for—"

"Don't." Letting out a huff of hot air, Dawn picked up her chair and sat back down. Once she'd wiped her teary face, she took a deep breath through her nose. "As I was going to say, Blake isn't pulling dinosaurs from the past." Unable to look either teenager in the eyes, she kept her gaze on the table. "He's been using his tele-drones on creatures SauraCorps had already brought to our present. All Blake does is gather them as he sees fit for his operations."

Viv placed a hand on Kam's back as he resumed sitting. "'Tele-drones' meaning teleportation, right?"

"Correct."

Though Kam had just been a target of Dr. Beaumont's wrath, a question pushed its way to the top of his mind. "How many drones does he have?"

Dawn chewed on her bottom lip.

"I'm assuming your silence means 'a lot'." Kam closed his eyes and let a small miffed laugh leave his mouth. "And I'm guessing dinosaurs aren't the only thing he's used them on?"

The quiet veterinarian picked up one of the electronic tablets.

Kam translated her body language in his author brain. "I'll take *that* as a 'no', too."

TWENTY-THREE

WITHIN HIS living quarters, Blake Arrowsmith took a generous sip of his afternoon Earl Grey tea. He placed the mug on a slate coaster before situating himself at his two-hundred-thousand-dollar wooden desk.

Removing the cellphone from his suit jacket, he reclined in his million-dollar, Italian-designed ergonomic desk chair.

Blake checked through his messages in one hand while rubbing the back of his neck with the other. Once he'd massaged his muscles enough, he picked up his tea for another taste.

He set the front side of his phone down.

His eyes closed for a moment.

A long, drawn-out breath flowed out of his lungs.

Dual computer monitors reflected a hazy distortion of himself. Another sip of tea rolled down his throat as he reached out and clicked the mouse. Both screens lit up.

Positioning his cursor on the right-hand screen, he

clicked a file folder.

Within that one, he clicked another icon.

Blake selected the first image in the list.

Every little tap of his finger on the right arrow key made more pictures slide into view. With every succeeding shot gracing his gaze, Blake subconsciously let his mouth turn into more of a grin.

Buzzzz. Buzzzz.

About to tap the keyboard once more, he reached out and picked up his phone.

The intel brought another smile to his face.

Kristjan Tómasson has been dealt with.

Having the phone in front of him, he noted the time in the top right-hand corner of the screen. He exited the messaging app and switched to his contacts. Typing in a name, he clicked on the person he wanted.

Ten seconds passed before the recipient picked up.

"Thought you said 'an hour'," Sebastian answered in annoyance.

"All in due *time*, Seb." Blake cleared his throat. "With what we've dealt with—rifts and all that—you should know."

Sebastian moved on to more important details. "Kids are still alive?"

"And kicking. Full of snark and attitude, as well as—"

"I'll take attitude over *ego* any day."

Blake chuckled. "Says the man who wanted to keep a

certain project all to himself."

Sebastian lowered his phone from his ear as he raised his voice in exasperation. "Oh my freaking God...." He brought the cellphone back up. "I still have to remind you of why? You wanted to take it to a level that it should never be taken to."

About to bring the cup of Earl Grey back to his lips, Blake halted. "Right, right, the whole *disrupting our timeline* you kept babbling on about."

Getting more worked up, Sebastian opted for a different angle. "Blake, you knew that back then.... Even today, I wish there was something I could do to help." He paused, hoping some compassion would make its way through to his old colleague. "Anything...*except this.*"

Arrowsmith took a victorious sip. "Good thing you now have an incentive."

"It was four years ago, Blake." Drenching his voice in empathy, Sebastian continued. "You could've moved on by—"

Slam!

The bottom of Blake's fist connected with the expensive African blackwood desk. "You bloody don't get it, Sebastian!" Wishing Sharpe stood in front of him to grab him by the neck, Blake growled. "You experienced what I had *all hopes for.*"

Sebastian had nothing he could respond with.

"At least you..." Blake gritted his teeth. "...had the chance to have *a family.*"

Silence was all Sebastian gave him.

Clenching his mobile, Blake failed to keep a tremor out of his voice. "And if you continue to deny me of that, then those *children* in my possession will *never* see theirs aga—"

"I have it."

Startled out of delivering his threat, Blake blinked a few times. To ease the roughness which grew within his throat, he took an unstable gulp of his tea. "Smart man."

"What do you want me to do now?" Sebastian's tone exhibited complete loss.

This time, Blake didn't say a word.

Getting anxious, Sebastian repeated himself. "What do you want me to—"

"Sit tight, Sharpe."

Arrowsmith ended the call.

The words that had been thrown back and forth had riled him up. Scratching the back of his head to relieve himself of some of the stress, he finished off the last of his now lukewarm drink.

Knock-knock-knock.

Blake reached for his mouse and clicked the image windows off of his computer screen. "Yes, come in."

A tanned man with a goatee entered, giving his superior a nod. "We're approaching the threshold."

Standing back up and running his hands down his suit, Blake nodded back to his Brazilian second in command. "In more ways than one, Felipe."

TWENTY-FOUR

"AT LEAST there's no dinosaur bits in salad. Hope this bacon isn't brachiosaurus." Fork in hand and alone with his girlfriend, Kamren tapped the pronged end among the leafy greens. "Peach vinaigrette is a nice touch."

Vivienne had only made it halfway through the meal of a salad. "Looks like we'll be vegans for our last meals."

Kam stopped chewing.

Her words rang around in his mind.

Last meals.

Adding gusto to his next chomp of kale and orange slices, he lowered his voice. "I was thinking…" He swallowed while planning a possible scenario. "…there may be a way off this thing."

Though there'd been a glint of hope in his voice, she kept her eyes on the bowl of food. "Kam, should we really get our hopes up?"

"Hear me out." He immediately dropped his fork into

his salad, allowing him to use both hands to emphasize his plan. "Beaumont mentioned the tele-drones. What if we could access one of them?"

Viv snorted. "You do remember the last time we decided to be reckless teens, it got us in a prehistoric pickle, right?"

"Mmm pickles, I could totally go for one."

"Dangit, same here. Sorry I mentioned it."

Kam resumed his thought process. "But say we find a drone. Maybe we could figure out a way to program it to teleport us home."

She looked at him with an arched eyebrow. "Do you honestly think programming a piece of high-tech machinery will be that easy?"

Kam gave her a cheeky grin. "We figured out iPads at the age of three, how hard could a drone—"

"Here's your luggage."

Whump!

Dawn had wheeled one of the bags over and plopped the other up on the table. "Might smell a bit like fruit, apparently they stored it with the food supplies."

"Yes!" Viv jumped up from her seat and rushed over. "Fresh clothes will help make things a bit more bearable."

"The SIM cards were removed from your phones, though." Dr. Beaumont made eye contact with Kam and nodded. "They didn't want you communicating with anyone. Can't give out the Wi-Fi password either."

Viv rolled her eyes. "Good Lord, I have nothing to live for now."

After snort-laughing at her over-the-top sarcasm, Kam

pointed his fork at Dawn while swallowing another bite of kale. "Thanks for getting those for us, and for *slamming* my head into the table earlier."

A surprised laugh slipped out of Dawn's mouth. "Don't mention it."

Shortly after their lunch, Kam and Viv had wheeled their luggage back to their room. Having their personal items back in their possession gave them a little boost.

Only one thing among Kam's belongings meant the most. *I can finally propose.*

Behind them, Phrodo had been following along. It pecked at each of their baggage along the way.

"Phrodo, what's gotten into you, buddy?" Viv called back to the dodo.

"There's nothing in these for you, birdie," Kam added while arriving at their door. Twisting the handle, he let his girlfriend enter first. "It's probably picking up the fruit smells or something."

"Whoa, really?" Once inside, Viv noticed the blow-up mattress in the middle of the room. Rolling her bag over beside it, she tsked. "How kind of them."

After allowing the dodo bird in, Kam strolled over to the other side. "If only they could do something about the music in this place."

"Ooooh, now that we have our phones back...." Viv unzipped a front flap on her bag and fished out her device.

She selected the music app on the main screen. "Battery's pretty low, but enough for something." Skipping the first couple of songs in her favorites list, she opted for one with a peppy beat: *Hypotheticals* by Lake Street Dive.

Kam couldn't resist bopping his head as he rested on the edge of the mattress. "Aw nice choice, babe."

Focusing so much on the happy song, Viv hadn't heard him.

Maneuvering from sitting to laying back, Kam audibly exhaled. "I can still call you babe, right?"

Inspecting a clean t-shirt, she turned to see her gloomy boyfriend staring at the dull ceiling. Taking advantage of being left completely alone—except for the dodo bird's presence—she ran her teeth over her bottom lip while choosing her words carefully. "Kamren, you need to understand that it takes me longer than you to process some things, okay?"

He went from gazing upward to down to his folded hands on his stomach.

"We both made our decisions that...*unfortunately* put us in this situation," she continued, admitting her own embarrassment. Perching herself on the air-bed, she reached across to place her hand on his chest. "Just...*please*...don't mistake my disappointment for hatred."

Kam closed his eyes. "If I hadn't offered our help, we wouldn't be fearing for our lives right now—"

"And I *need* you to know that I *don't* and *will never* hate you for that." She lifted her hand and placed it onto his cheek. "I mean, yeah, this all sucks. But at least dinosaurs won't attack us on this boat, at least I hope not."

"Now that's a *Jaws* movie I'd go see." Kam smirked, turning over and kissing her palm. "Probably be a good date night movie."

"I'll pass, because nightmares." Viv flicked his nose. "I'd drag you to a rom-com."

He chuckled at the visual. "You mean you'd still date me after all of this?"

With a playful smirk, she leaned over and pressed her lips into his for a couple seconds. Letting her nose brush against his, she whispered, "How's that for an answer?"

He closed one eye and cocked his head to the side. "Hmm, might need some *extra clarification* on that."

Viv snort-laughed before sliding off the mattress. "Let me change out of these gross clothes first. We passed by a bathroom on our way, right?"

"Should be near the end of the hall."

Still smelling fruit from Kam's travel bag, Phrodo used its beak to wedge the zipper open.

Clean clothing in hand, Viv opened the door and flicked the rubber stop down. "Should air out this room, too. Get rid of the boat-stank."

Once she left the room, Kam embraced a surge of confidence and awkwardly shuffled to get off the blow-up mattress.

Head-deep into the teen's luggage, Phrodo's curious coos were muffled by clothing.

"Get outta there, dude." Kam pulled the bird back and opened the main flap all the way. Digging through everything, he finally came to his suit jacket. *I have to do this tonight. Might not get another chance.* He thrust his hand into the inner breast pocket.

Empty.

"What?"

Flinging all the other clothes right out of the way, he picked up the jacket and shook it.

Nothing made any clunky noise.

"But it's… I put it—"

Dooo-dooo.

Kam glanced back. "Quiet down, I'm trying to…."

He shifted his feet to look directly at the dodo.

Phrodo simply stood in the doorway.

The ring box sat cradled in its beak.

Kam lifted his arm to begin reaching for the jewelry. *"Phrodo,* that isn't food, bud—"

Dooo-dooo!

Gone.

Phrodo had dashed down the hallway.

"Why?" Eyes wide open, Kam bolted for the door. "Someone please tell me *why?!"*

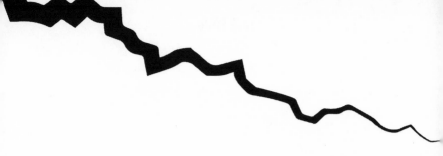

TWENTY-FIVE

"PHRODO!"

Dashing through the open doorway, Kamren grabbed onto the left side frame and swung himself into the hallway.

Further down, Phrodo speed-waddled around a corner.

Kam shook his head as he ran. "This is the most ridiculous—"

"What are you doing?" Dawn called down from behind him.

"The *bird's* got *the ring!*"

Kam didn't look back to see if the veterinarian had joined in the chase. He kept his eyes forward, determined to stop the oblivious dodo from thwarting his proposal plans.

As he turned the corner, he found Phrodo tapping the box against the floor.

"Phrodo, buddy, listen to me." Slowing his steps to try and keep the bird still, he readied his hands in case he needed to lunge. "Please be careful with that thing."

Crackle!

Phrodo engaged its beak to work the little black cardboard box like a large nut.

Kam tensed up. "Are…you trying to open—"

Crack-pop!

The spine of the box gave way to the dodo's sturdy bill.

A sterling silver circle with diamonds attached tumbled to the hallway floor.

Kam's gaze snapped downward to the jewelry.

Noticing the sparkly item, Phrodo tossed the broken box aside and gawked back and forth with both eyes.

Only a few feet away from the bird, Kam left his mouth open. "I swear, if you ruin this for me, I will serve you with cranberry sauce."

The hooked tip of the dodo's upper beak shuffled the ring forward a tad before gingerly picking it up.

Nervous about making any sudden movements, Kam froze. "Want me to add gravy and stuffing on the side?"

Dooo-dooo.

Phrodo backed away, not letting go of the jewelry.

"Can't believe I'm about to make this reference." Kam stared right into the dodo's black eyes. "Phrodo…*give me the ring.*"

Dawn came around the corner. "Why are you chasing the dodo?"

Kam didn't take his gaze off the bird. "Uh…well…as you can see, Phrodo has given in to the power of the ring."

"Excuse me?" Trying to get a clearer picture, she came up beside him. "What's it—"

"Don't scare it!" Kam put an arm up to block her, breaking his concentration. "It has the ring I need to give to Viv."

Dawn studied the feathered creature. "Oh no."

Eyes back on Phrodo, Kam noted the closed beak. "No."

Dooo-dooo.

"No, Phrodo, did you—"

Dooo-dooo

"No…no…*noooo!*" Kam staggered forward, his weakened knees bringing him to the linoleum. Everything he'd hoped for now sat within the dodo bird's stomach. Though the hallway seemed to go topsy-turvy in his mind, he witnessed the dodo waddling up to him in innocence. "Phrodo… you…*ate* the ring?"

Dooo-dooo-dooo.

Off to the side, Dawn placed a hand to her mouth to suppress a chuckle. "Hopefully it passes through."

Kam raised a hand, ready to strike the bird in utter exasperation, when it rubbed its feathered head against his torso. He lowered the hand, letting it rest on the dodo's head. "Guess I'm keeping you close from now on. That'll be one expensive crap."

Dressed in fresh clean clothes, Viv approached the mirror in the bathroom. She scratched at her scalp while running her fingers through her hair. Part of her wanted to linger there as if it were a pocket of serenity within the despicable Arrowsmith's ship.

Her throat became scratchy and closed up as she focused on the dismal circumstances. Wishing her mind had stronger defenses, she winced as Blake's words pierced right through.

"I'll still dangle you in front of Sebastian for what I need, then you'll be disposed *of."*

Shivers crawled up and down her back as it tensed.

Fearing for her life wasn't a new feeling by any means.

She'd been thrown through a rift to dinosaur times.

A massive millipede could have ended her.

Her fingers had slipped through Kam's while battling the current of a raging river.

Stepping on an egg had nearly led to a therizinosaurus' scythe-like claw gutting her.

The chaos of the giganotosaurus nesting grounds had turned all of her danger meters to an all-time high.

Her outstretched hand had been inches away from a closing rift, cutting her off from the love of her life.

Though Kam had found a way home, the initial sense of loss had given Viv a mean gut-punch.

Waking up in a dark carrier bin on a gigantic boat had begun the spiral once more.

Droplets of tears landed on her shirt, turning the shade of green slightly darker.

Among the anxious thoughts, she closed her eyes and forced herself to keep one thing constant in her mind. The only thing that had kept her going through all those events.

Kamren.

His lightheartedness and sense of humor had kept her

mostly sane through everything that had happened about a year ago. He'd also sacrificed himself to the prehistoric world, pushing her through the time rift to make sure she'd get home first.

Though Kamren's actions had led to them being trapped on a vessel in open waters, she still had him by her side.

I'll always need him by my side.

The more she thought about him, the more she considered his feelings. She'd been so focused on herself taking in and processing everything that she hadn't considered how he'd been fairing.

Wonder if he's actually as freaked out as I am under all those quips.... A little smile grew on her face, since she'd always loved his sense of humor—as cheesy as it was sometimes. *Would probably do us good to have a talk minus animosity.*

After scooping up her dirty clothes, she headed for the door.

Doorknob in hand, she took a deep breath.

"Hey, Perry, got a minute?" someone called over to another person a few feet away.

"What's going on, Rutherford?" the other man responded.

Instead of leaving the bathroom, Viv kept the door open a crack to avoid Arrowsmith's employees.

"Unless you heard already..." Rutherford glanced down each direction of the hallway. "...Arrowsmith's last deal with Tómasson, uh...*fell through*. We'll need your help with rounding up some assets tomorrow."

"At home base?"

"Yep, after arrival, we'll be selling the majority off for

food orders," Rutherford explained with pure indifference. "Someone even wants to see if baby mammoth is like veal."

Perry made a hungry sound. "Bet you it'd be good ground up for burgers."

"We should go grab a bite." Rutherford gave his friend's shoulder a backhanded tap. "It'd be good to catch up."

Once the two men's footsteps couldn't be heard anymore, Viv exited the bathroom. Although, hearing of the baby mammoth Downey being sold for someone to butcher made her stomach threaten to send her back to the toilet.

"These people are…absolutely *sickening.*"

"Getting sea sick?" Dawn asked from behind her. "I should have some—"

"Oh yeah, it's *definitely 'the water'* making me sick while everyone who works for your *revolting* boyfriend are all accomplices to animal murder." Viv blew past the veterinarian on her way back to the makeshift bedroom. She stopped at the doorway and half-turned. "They better not touch Downey."

"Downey…the mammoth calf?" Dawn flexed her hands hanging at her sides.

Kam smirked at Phrodo entering their room as he came up beside his girlfriend. "Something happen to the fluffy little guy?"

About to pull him into the room by the arm, Viv raised her voice at Dr. Beaumont. "Tell Blake if he so much as touches a strand of wool on that mammoth…."

Unease rose within Kam as he noted infuriation in her eyes. "Viv, tell me what's—whoa-jeez!"

Wham!

Viv had yanked him inside and slammed the door.

Out in the hall, Dawn stood motionless other than her lungs starting to work double-time. She shoved a hand into her pant pocket, pulled out her phone, and unlocked the screen.

Her fingers flew to the messaging app, pulled up a conversation, and began typing:

Call me. We have a situation.

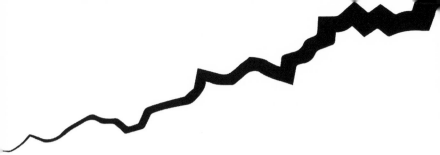

TWENTY-SIX

MARCHING WITH tenacity, Dawn came upon Blake's living quarters and didn't knock before entering.

Glancing up from his computer, Blake smiled. "Afternoon, my dear."

"Did you get my message?"

He lit up his phone's screen with a couple taps of his finger. "Sorry, love, I've been catching up with e-mails and the like." Standing up to stretch, he met her halfway and caressed her cheek with his palm. "What's the matter?"

A bothered sigh exited her mouth. "It's those kids."

"What about them?"

She leaned into his hand and gazed down at the rustic hardwood flooring. "Maybe it's the maternal instinct finally coming out of me, but I don't know if I can face having to harm them when the time comes."

"Oh, sweetie." Blake slid his hand down to the top of her shoulder. "If it will make you feel any better, I can assign

Felipe to them."

Hearing the Brazilian's name made her uncomfortable. "Do we really have to kill them? They're just out of high schoo—"

"Dawn, they've seen me, they've seen what we do on this vessel," he countered, waving his hand around the room. "Any set of eyes on my operation either works for me or doesn't live to tell about it."

Flexing the muscles in her jaw, she nodded as she fitted her body up against his. "I'm… I'm sorry, I know I shouldn't worry about them."

"Listen, sweetheart, caring never makes anyone a bad person." Admiration emanated through his voice as he kissed her forehead. "I care *deeply* about you."

She soaked up his embrace and came in for a kiss. "I don't deserve how good you've treated me."

"Oh, come now." He grinned and rubbed his nose against hers. "You make it quite easy to be good to you."

Dawn kissed him again, snagging his bottom lip for a moment. "I'd love to stick around…but I should get back to those teenage inconveniences."

Before she could walk away, Blake gripped her wrist, directing her back to him. "Breaks are allowed, you know. Especially if it's with me."

She leaned in close, keeping her lips an inch away from his. "We'll have a nice moment later, lovey."

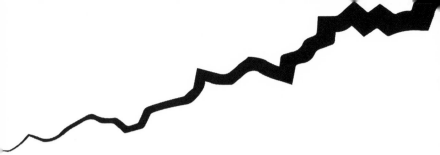

TWENTY-SEVEN

SETTLED ON the foot of the mattress, Kamren watched his unsettled girlfriend pacing back and forth in their 'assigned room'. "Babe, what's got you all worked up?"

"Because…." Vivienne broke her march and rubbed her face. "I don't even know what to say because it'll end up with you saying, 'I told you so.'"

"Okay?" Intrigued, he raised his right eyebrow. "Then let's talk through what you're—"

"Yes, I chose to help Phrodo," Viv started out, placing both hands on her hips while looking at the dodo. "And that was the first domino which led us on the path of ending up here."

"And when I saw that sense of justice in you, it made me love you more." Kam spoke in admiration, smiling as he did so. "I'm sorry I threw that in your face earlier."

She lost control of her breathing pattern. "But when I… I heard those men talking…about selling off most of the animals on this ship...*for food?* No one here *cares* about these living things."

Kam stood up when he heard her voice's instability intensifying. "Vivienne." His hands slid past her shoulders as he enveloped her in an embrace. When she nuzzled her face into the crook of his neck, he squeezed her tighter. "But you care, and I *admire* that."

Whimpering, she loosened her grip on him to turn her head away from him. "Then I scolded you for wanting to help Sebastian."

"Hey." Kam laid his left hand against her cheek. His thumb rubbed a tear away as he turned her face back to his. "It's not every day someone kidnaps you and throws you in a C-bin on a boat. Our emotions got out of hand earlier."

Her gaze zig-zagged up and down from his kind eyes to his mouth. "This is when you're supposed to say, 'I told you so.'"

Grinning, he kissed her forehead. "Blame games hurt relationships. We need to be *united* on this rig."

By now, Viv sensed her body starting to relax as they hugged. "I've been so wrapped up in how everything's affecting me, I haven't even considered how you've been doing with all of this."

Taking a deep breath, he glanced away for a moment. "I mean, you know...dire situations bring the humor and pop culture references out of me."

She released an involuntary chuckle. "But behind those coping mechanisms, how are you really doing?"

As much as he wanted to keep squeezing her, he stepped

away. "There's a mix." He glanced down at Phrodo, who had kept unusually quiet during the heart-to-heart. "I figured trying to stand up for what I thought was right would show you that I don't always freeze like 'a popsicle.'"

Deep down, Viv regretted ever calling him that. "Kamren, you know I don't—"

"And if I hadn't worried so damn much of how you thought of me in that way…" He ran a hand through his hair before turning it into a fist and leaning against the wall. "…we wouldn't have ended up in this precarious position."

She stepped forward and grabbed onto his shirt with both hands. "You've never had to prove your manliness to me." Being closer, she let go of his clothes and draped her arms around his neck. "Because I've only ever loved you as the man you are already."

About to respond, Kam let out a breath of rich relief. "And…I want to be your man *forever*—"

Vivienne pressed her lips into his, cutting him off. All of her pent-up anxious energy flooded from her brain to her heart where it converted into passion.

Kissing her back, Kam gave in to tingling heat overtaking his entire body. With his arms clasped around her, his lips against hers, and sensing her heart beating as fast as his own, somehow he found the power within to pull his face away. "Viv, I *need*—"

She came at him with another kiss.

"As *incredibly hot* as this—"

Her fingers had taken hold of his hair, coercing his mouth back to hers.

He groaned while forcing himself back. "Listen, I need to ask you something really important before I miss my chance."

Disappointed, Viv wiped her mouth with the back of her wrist. "You'd rather ask me a question than have a make-out sesh?"

Taking her reasoning into account, he stepped forward. "I mean, we clearly need this."

"Heck yeah we do."

As soon as her left hand grabbed onto his, Kam immediately thought of a specific finger of hers missing a certain something. "Okay, but before the sesh...." He bent over and scooped both hands under the dodo bird's feathered belly.

Confused and slightly amused, Viv snorted. "Why are you picking up Phrodo?"

While turning around, Kam couldn't hold back a blissful smile. "This isn't at all how I imagined this would go down but...."

Buzzzzzz. Buzzzzzz.

A generic ringtone sounded from somewhere in their room.

The surprising noise yanked both of the teens out of the moment.

"That..." Viv tilted her head as if to pinpoint the location of the ringing. "...isn't one of our phones, Beaumont said the SIM cards were removed."

In mid-knee-bend, Kam lowered his head at the mysterious cellphone foiling his plan. "It's like I'm in a story where the author hates me."

Cradled in the human's hands, Phrodo turned its head to look at Kam.

Dooo-dooo-dooo.

"Quirky animal sidekick, check."

Detecting the phone's jingle coming from Kam's luggage bag, Viv opened it up and dug her hand around the bottom past the clothing. "What the?" She revealed the gadget. "This *isn't* yours."

Kam set the dodo back down. "Should we answer it?"

"It keeps ringing, I don't know—"

"I'll do it." He held out his palm. "Not because I'm trying to be manly, just to be clear."

Viv let him take it, then picked at her thumb cuticle. "I hope no one catches us with—"

"Hello?" Kam had opened the flip phone and accepted the call. "Who's—"

"Kamren? Is that you?"

Squinting, the teen picked up on recognizable inflections. *"Sharpe?"*

Sebastian made a quick response. "Is Viv there with you?"

"Uh, yeah, she's right here," Kam answered, enabling the speakerphone option. "Wait, is this a burner phone or some—"

"Are you coming to *save* us?" Viv stared at the little speaker with eagerness.

"Sorry, Vivienne," Sebastian replied, sorrow in his voice. "I'm doing all I can, but I'm still in the dark on a lot of how Blake operates. Speaking of, we don't have much time." Urgency took centerstage in his tone. "You're getting closer to his base of operations, and I need you two to do something for me."

Rather than jump at the opportunity to help, this time Kam looked into his girlfriend's eyes. He hoped to not get her into more trouble than they already were.

She held onto his arm and gave a permissive nod. "As long as we do it together."

Kamren brought the phone closer to his mischievous grin. "Are you about to make us double-oh-sevens?"

"Not quite. I need you to create a diversion."

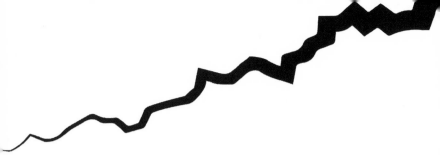

TWENTY-EIGHT

MINUTES LATER, the two teens snuck out into the hallway.

They'd gone over details with Sebastian twice, making sure things would hopefully go better than their previous assignment.

Last time ended with them getting pumped full of tranquilizer and in Arrowsmith's confinement.

Kamren detained Phrodo within their room as he closed the door with stealth. By doing so, he also kept the engagement ring safe. He then took the lead toward their destination.

"Someone on this boat must be working with Sebastian." Vivienne maintained a lowered voice to avoid attention. "Like a double agent."

Ahead of her by a couple steps, Kam brushed a hand past his pocket, doublechecking that he'd kept the burner phone on him. "Makes sense, I'm surprised he didn't say who."

As they traversed forward, she attempted putting some pieces together. "Could've been anyone who's had access to our luggage."

Kam glanced around the corner. "With how successful Arrowsmith's been, you'd think he would've smelled a rat by now."

Viv followed him down a set of stairs. "Wait, *Beaumont* brought us our bags, what if she's the—"

"And went WWE on my head, remember?"

"Well, if she *is* the one, she wouldn't want her cover blown—"

"She opted to spike my head like a friggin' volleyball."

Viv chuckled at his analogy as they came to the bottom of the stairs. "Sounds like your ego got bruised, too."

"Perhaps." Closing in on the creature containment room, Kam checked the hallway up and down. "And the coast… seems to be…clear."

They dashed across to the damaged doorway. Simply sneaking through the opening where one of the doors used to be, they kept their steps as silent as possible. As they shuffled past cages of all sizes, some prehistoric creatures made groans while others chittered.

"Hope these guys don't give us away." Viv kept an eye out for Arrowsmith's men. "Are we close to it yet?"

"I don't see it in this bay." Kam led them past a barred enclosure which held an ankylosaur. "Hey, it's a club-tailed dino."

"Gawk later." Viv pushed him on. "Find the dinosaur we need first."

In one of the cages near the end, a full-grown therapod sat on the floor with its head and tail curled toward each other.

Viv noted the name written on a whiteboard attached to the outside. "This is the one, right?"

"Mega… Yep, this is it." Kam hurried over to a keypad, pulled out the burner phone, and dialed. "We're ready to *'Lost World'* this dino."

"Good, wait…." On the other end, Sebastian paused. "*'Lost World'?*"

"The Jurassic Park sequel. The evil dudes have dinos locked up and Vince Vaughn shows up with bolt cutters to let all the dinos loose—"

"Not the time to explain movie plot points." Viv rushed over to her boyfriend's side and stared at the buttons. "What's the code?"

Sebastian heard her through the device's tiny microphone. "It should be zero-four-one-eight—"

"What do *you two* think you're *doing?*"

Kam and Viv turned around.

Dr. Beaumont stood about ten feet behind them.

She pointed a loaded gun at the teens. "Don't make me ask again."

"Guess that answers your question," Kam directed at Viv. "Listen, Dawn, we were—"

"Did you *really* think I would take my eyes off you?" Dawn kept the weapon raised while scolding them. "Get back to your room, *now.*"

Sebastian could only hear parts of the dialog. "Who is

that? What's going on?"

Viv made shallow breaths as she grabbed onto Kam's right arm. "She's right, we should go—"

"No." He forced down an apprehensive lump in his throat. "We're going to see this through."

Just as surprised as Viv, Dawn's eyes flared open even more. "Don't be *stupid* about this."

Leaving his girlfriend's side, Kam stepped toward the veterinarian. "Viv and I are doomed either way, right? Be a part of Blake's plan, he kills us. Try and stop him while we're here, he'll still kill us."

Viv couldn't believe his sudden moment of brazen courage. It reminded her of when he'd challenged Emily-Ann a year ago. *"Kamren, why—"*

"Back away, Kam." Dawn tightened her grip on the gun. "This doesn't have to get—"

"If we die trying to stop Arrowsmith, then we'll die doing the right thing." Sweat formed on his face as he stared down the barrel of her semi-automatic. His next step brought his forehead to the muzzle. "So just *do it* already."

"Kamren, *stop it!*" Terror coursed through Viv as she reached out while her legs stayed fixed in place. "Don't do this!"

Dawn hardened her stare. "Listen to your girl—"

"Get it over with," Kam whimpered as a tear streaked down his left cheek. With the gun still against his head, he barely shook his head side to side. "If I can't live a life with *her* by my side, then there's…no life worth living."

Behind him, Viv faltered in keeping her weeping discreet.

Hearing his words made her heart swell and shatter as if it'd been hit by a bullet.

On the handle side of the gun, Dawn slowly opened her mouth, but couldn't form the words to say in return.

Tilting himself forward, Kam closed his eyes as he sniffled.

Dawn's forearm twitched as she whipped her gaze side to side.

"Cover your ears."

Shocked, Kam opened his eyes. *"What?"*

Dr. Beaumont repeated what she'd whispered. "Cover your ears."

Dropping the phone to place his palms over his ears, Kam lowered his jaw in disbelief. "The heck are you—"

KA-BLAM-BLAM!

Viv jumped back a step as the bullets struck the keypad. Looking back at the woman, she remained absolutely speechless.

"You...." Kam lowered his hands, though his ears still rang a bit. "You... You're...."

Taking advantage while the stunned teenager stood there, Dawn snatched the phone from the floor. "Hey, Sebastian."

"Beaumont!" The SauraCorps owner spoke with relief. "Are Kam and Viv all right?"

"They're alive, but a little shaken up," she reported, slipping the handgun into the back of the waistband of her pants. "But the mission is still a go."

TWENTY-NINE

"YOU...." **STILL** coming to terms over a couple of bullets blasting off beside his head, Kamren couldn't move. "This whole freaking time?"

Leaving the cage bars behind her, Vivienne managed to pull herself toward her alive boyfriend. "Kamren, are you okay?" Then she gave Dr. Beaumont a wild glare. "After everything you've put us through—"

"I'm sure my apologies won't be able to cover it all." Dawn held the phone back out to the teenage boy. "Things had to go a certain way to make it convincing."

Viv placed both of her hands on Kam's shoulders. "So naturally, you *had to* tranq us *and* beat him up."

Aware of the gunshots bringing possible attention to their position, Dawn inspected all around them. "With Arrowsmith watching my moves, I did what I had to."

"Riiiiiight." Kam eventually grabbed the phone. "You didn't choose the dino-spy life, the dino-spy life chose you."

"Hey!" A voice called out into the containment room. "Who's shooting?"

As the two teens and veterinarian united in silence, they looked back toward the imprisoned dinosaur.

Awakened from its nap, the prehistoric creature peered down at the humans with inquisitive, reptilian eyes.

"Megalosaurus, huh?" Fascinated by its stature, Dawn opened the cage door all the way. "Zero-four-one-eight-nine is the full code. Let's go open some more."

Three of Arrowsmith's people began sweeping through the ship's inner room. Rifles up and loaded, they checked on each of the animals along the way. At the midway point, they came upon smaller cages and crates lined up back-to-back in the middle.

"You sure it was gunshots, Dockery?" one of them asked.

"How much you guys wanna bet it was Andrew?" Dockery laughed, shaking her ponytail as it poked out the back of her black ballcap. "Probably picked off one of the compy's, since one of them nipped his ankle—"

RRRROOOOOOOAAAAAARRRR!

The hulking megalosaurus sprinted forward.

Before anyone could take aim, the dinosaur rammed its head into one of the operatives. It snagged another by their tactical outfit with its front teeth and whipped them upward into the metallic ceiling.

Dockery dropped to the floor to avoid detection. She

ducked behind some crates and scrambled for her walkie-talkie. "Code: Orange, I repeat, *Code: Orange!* One of the assets is out of...."

She glanced over at the half of a doorway.

A pack of five turkey-sized velociraptors scurried through it.

Further down, a pair of pterodactyl infants nudged their cage door open, crawled onto the top of their enclosure, and stretched out their wings.

"Dammit." She hadn't taken her thumb off the Push-To-Talk button. "We need more hands on this. *Multiple assets are....*"

Dagger-like teeth entered Dockery's left peripheral view.

The megalosaurus brought its scrutinizing eye closer.

Recalling her facial details and specific scent, it recognized her as part of the earlier crew which had 'welcomed' it with tranquilizers and electric prods.

Therefore, it viewed her as a threat.

Dockery's chin trembled. "Oh God. The megalosaurus is—*AAAAUUUUGH!*"

"Hopefully that keeps them busy for a while." Dawn led the teens up to the top level.

Kamren stayed behind Vivienne, making sure she'd be safe. "What exactly are we trying to keep them busy *from?*"

Heading down the hall a few steps and over to a window, Dawn placed a hand on the wall while gazing out. She cursed under her breath. "Less movement among the boat is generally better once we get to this point."

Viv subconsciously shuffled toward the next window down. "Are those clouds supposed to look like that?"

"Clouds?" Kam strode over to see for himself. "Like funky animal shapes, or…." As soon as the sky came into view for him, he held his breath.

"Are we…." Viv slipped her hand into his. "Is it what I think it—"

Letting go of her hand, Kam marched over to the nearest access to outside.

Dawn started after him. "Kamren, we need to stay inside."

Before she could finish, he'd already stepped out.

A decent gust of wind ruffled his hair.

Above, purplish and reddish hues glowed among the cloudy atmosphere. Fierce bolts of crackling electricity shot all around, glowing, dissipating, then sparking to life all over again. It formed an ominous wall from the water's surface up to the stratosphere.

In absolute awe of the phenomenon, Kam barely took his eyes off it when Viv joined him on the walkway.

"It's like someone infused a sunset into a thunderstorm," she remarked, sucking in a deep breath as she took it all in. "Then doused them with steroids."

Dawn remained at the door as she called out to them. "Pretty soon it won't be safe out here. Come on back—"

"What *is* this?" Kam didn't look back.

Streaks of lightning zig-zagged all directions along the

mass of daunting cloud.

With her hand on the railing, Viv shivered as her arm hairs stood up. "We've seen electrical currents like those before."

"But this…." Dumbfounded by the breathtaking yet threatening stationary storm, Kam slowly raised a pointed finger. "This is way…*way bigger.*"

Against her own judgement, Dawn joined them. "The world knows about the Bermuda Triangle, but few have actually visited it."

Her words registered in Viv's ears. "Excuse me?" She pried her gaze away to give Dr. Beaumont haphazard glances. "That is the *actual…Bermuda…Triangle?*"

Dawn nodded. "We're approaching one of its borders, actually."

"Also known as 'The *Devil's* Triangle'," Kam brought up, alarm overtaking his matter-of-fact tone. "Perfect place for someone like Arrowsmith."

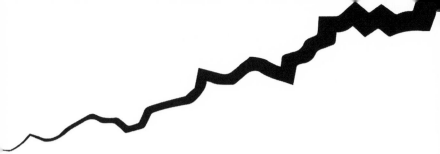

THIRTY

BLAKE ENTERED the vessel's cockpit with exasperation in his step and expression. He stomped straight over to his attentive navigator. "Ashbury, mind telling me why we're slowing down?"

She did her best to hide her fear. "Assets are loose on the ship. You know as well as I do, if there's too much activity—"

"We managed to subdue the megalosaurus earlier and people are on their way to do it again," he snapped back, barely connecting his gaze with hers.

The turbulent spectacle ahead had captured his full attention.

"There's more running free than just the mega—"

"Then I'll order kill shots." Blake had already taken his phone out. *"Keep* us on track, Heather. Timing is *crucial* at this point."

A text message from Felipe popped up:

She's in position.

He stepped away from the semi-reluctant navigator, focusing on the smartphone's screen. Rubbing his tongue over the sharp ridges of his molars, he zoomed in on a map with tense fingers. *Timing is everything.*

Beer in hand, Sebastian reclined on a stool at his kitchen island. He'd been waiting for further instruction from Blake for longer than he'd expected.

Felicia popped a cork out of a wine bottle. "Are you sure there's no other way?"

Sebastian closed his eyes as he took another swig. "He's always been an absolute pain to deal with." He tilted the head of his beer bottle at her. "Remember trying to work out old SauraCorps deals where he was involved?"

"Oh God. He'd claimed he did more work and deserved more of the cut." Felicia lingered on the red wine's berry and leathery aromatics. "I bet you he owed everyone a billion favors, and he always got away with it."

"Which is why…" Sebastian brought the bottle's top to his lips, but didn't sip. "…no matter what, I can't let him do any more harm."

Felicia sat in the stool beside him. Once she'd set the wineglass down, she layered her left hand over his. "I'm horrible at this, but…."

Sensing a worry in her voice, he shifted on his seat.

"Felicia, I will do *everything* I can to talk him down."

"And if talking doesn't work?"

"Then…."

She pierced her fretful gaze into his eyes. "Then it becomes a possible *suicide mission,* and I can't—"

"You'll be fine," he responded with a hopeful half-smile, though his voice gave away his own qualms. "In case anything happens to me, everything will be taken care of. Aiden and Olivia…they're still growing to love you."

"And you expect me to be fine looking after all of this?" Glancing to the French doors which opened up to a patio, she could see long-necked dinosaurs off in the distance. "I'm already overwhelmed as it is."

"It will all be looked after." He rubbed the top of her hand before kissing it. "If what I'm about to do saves you, the kids, and the dinosaurs…then so be it."

Plucking a napkin from the center of the island, she wiped her ruined mascara from under her eyes. "Seb, we've only *just started* this…" She wagged her hand back and forth from her to him. "…and I *can't lose* you like…."

Buzzzz. Buzzzz.

Overcome with tears, Sebastian whispered an apology before wrenching his gaze away from his distraught partner.

One of his own employees had been calling.

Phone to his ear, he spoke. "Hey, Carson, uh… can I call you back?"

"Are you inside?"

Sebastian wiped his blurred eyes with his sleeve. "I am, but I—"

"Oh my—everyone, *get down!*"

Felicia heard the shout through the phone's mic.

Already off the stool, Sebastian started for the kitchen doors. "What the heck's going on out—"

KER-SMASH!

Wood splintered and shards of glass sprayed inward.

Felicia shrieked as Sebastian fell backward to the tile floor.

A bulky, humming piece of tech had barged in.

ZEEUU-ZEEUU-ZEEUU.

"Dammit." Sebastian tried to pick himself up, but his hand slipped on a fragment of glass. "He made me a sitting duck in my own—"

ZEEUU-BWOOOOM!

Space-time energy teleported him away.

Frazzled, Felicia feared the whirring drone. It had taken the man she'd grown to love with such power and ease.

Gone in an instant of time.

The drone powered down. It crunched into the tiles where Sebastian had once been. Engine hums faded as lights flickered on and off until they finally expired.

"My God." Felicia stepped toward the hunk of immobilized machinery. "Blake's really doing this."

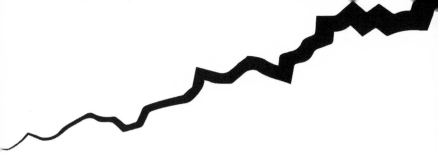

THIRTY-ONE

MOLECULE BY molecule, Sebastian teleported to a rubber-matted floor. Still on his back, he glanced all around. *Is this his ship?* After checking his left, he looked over his shoulder.

Teeth sat inches from his face.

An unconscious megalosaurus took labored breaths.

Scrambling back to his feet, he nearly bumped into the barrels of multiple rifles.

"Jeez." Sebastian put his hands right up to show his compliance. As he noticed certain facial details on each of the personnel, he began recognizing each of them from files he'd scoured concerning Arrowsmith's operations. He also recalled their bank statements. "Listen, guys, whatever Blake's paying you, I can more than double—"

"Not even here a full minute and you're already trying to bribe my men?" Blake came from behind his guards and approached his old workmate. "Money isn't the only thing that…*encourages* people to work for me."

As Sebastian's adrenaline subsided, he glanced back at the tranquilized megalosaurus. "Seeing as you kidnap people, guess I wouldn't put anything else past you."

Blake laughed with sinister foreboding. "If I remember correctly, you used to be fairly proficient at living among gray lines."

Letting his hands sink to his sides, Sebastian made a subtle nod to himself. "Until I realized gray lines are the lies that help us sleep at night."

About to retort, Blake simply twitched the corner of his mouth up for a split-second.

In response to the tell, Sebastian flicked an eyebrow up. "Still waking up at three AM screaming out her name, then, huh—"

THWACK!

Blake's fist came through like a bullet.

Dazed and back to the floor, Sebastian grumbled before spitting out a gob of blood onto the rubber mats.

After straightening his suit, Blake crouched and slung an arm under his former friend's armpit. "Come along, old friend." He began leading him off whether Sharpe's legs wanted to work or not. "I'm sure we'd have a thrilling conversation over ethics, but I wouldn't want you to miss the show."

"Hold up." As Kamren passed each window, his eyes were

constantly drawn to the space-time storm. "Arrowsmith *wants* to go toward that thing?"

Taking cautious steps ahead of the teens, Dawn held up a hand to them as she neared a corner. "He's done it many times before."

Vivienne caught herself staring at the monstrous anomaly. "So there's something on the other side?"

"Let's keep moving." Dawn waved them on, attentive to every angle and noise along the way. "And yes, we're heading toward his—"

"Stop right there!" An unfamiliar and heavily accented voice yelled toward them.

Up ahead, a man entered their line of sight.

Neither Viv nor Kam knew who he was.

As for Dawn, she placed a hand on her hip—close to her gun. "Felipe, what's going on?"

"Dinosaurs are loose on the ship." Felipe already had a semi-automatic gun in his hand as he advanced toward them. "Someone reported gunshots. Any idea of who that might've been?"

Kam tsked into a laugh. "Dude, literally *everyone* on this boat has a gun except for us."

Nodding his head to the side, Felipe slipped the weapon back into its chest harness holder. "Fair point." Wagging a finger at the veterinarian, he continued. "Since you're here, Dawn, Blake wants to see you on the bridge."

She feigned concern. "Is something wrong?"

"He wanted to make sure you were safe as we go through the storm." Felipe scratched at his chin's stubble. "Kids can come, too."

Viv glanced from the window to the man, then back to the captivating clouds. "Great. Because I wanted a better vantage point."

Dawn chuckled. "You remind me so much of my daughter."

"And here we are." Blake entered the cockpit, then held the door open for his former colleague. "The best view in the house."

Each step Sebastian took slowed until he came to a complete stop.

From left to right, the tempered glass offered a massive view of the ethereal space-time tempest. A nonstop churning of thick, electrified clouds took up the entirety of the windows.

KA-KA-KA-KA-BRRRRUUUUM!

Super-charged thunder shook the entire cabin.

"Ooooh, she's an angry one this time," Blake remarked, standing right in the middle of the panes. "Full steam ahead, Ashbury."

Agitation struck Sebastian in the stomach and took form as sirens wailing in his mind. "We're going into it?"

Arrowsmith simply held his own hand behind his back. "That's always been one of your flaws, Seb. Amazing discoveries have been within your grasp, yet you've always played it safe."

On the opposite side of the cockpit, Dawn stepped through with the teens right behind her. "Blake, you called for—" As soon as her eyes met Sebastian's, she fought to keep herself in a natural stride.

Unprepared to see her in the same room as Blake, Sebastian went into improvisation mode. "Beaumont? I thought you were—"

"Sebastian!" Vivienne heard his voice and grinned. "You're... Wait, how did you even get here?"

"Excellent." Blake spoke up to be louder than everyone else. "The whole lot of you are here to witness greatness."

Kam squinted at the Englishman. "Well, I was hoping to go to an *Aerosmith* concert, guess I'm at the wrong—*oof!*"

Viv had smacked him in the lower abdominals. "What have I said about that?"

With a passive smile, Blake left his position by the windows. "I'm happy you're all here to see this gorgeous spectacle." He pointed to it with an open palm. "No one knows how long this space-time energy has been surging so miraculously here. Some believe it's been active since the dawn of time itself, providing access to times past."

Hanging on to every word, Viv considered the history of the mystifying Bermuda Triangle. "So the stories are true? All those lost ships and...Amelia Earhart?"

"Does that mean William Shakespeare was right, too?" Kam brought up, pulling from his knowledge of written works.

"'*The Tempest*'. Impressive, boy," Blake added as he neared Dawn's side. "And yes, many have entered and been lost from the world. Until a year ago, when SauraCorps literally imploded. Choices were made, and some of us were left to pick up our own pieces and find a way to move on. As for me, I hired some of the best minds in the world to study this." His gaze went back to the magnificent view. "Stealing some of Xing's tech helped, of course. We took his anti-rift energy bombs and found a way to create, well…. How long until the diffusion shields are up, Heather?"

"About two minutes."

"Perfect." Blake rubbed his hand around Dawn's back. "Just enough time to take care of a few *things!*"

Dawn yelped as he snatched the back of her hair, allowing him to seize the gun from her waist with ease.

Guarding the door, Felipe unholstered his gun and monitored everyone else.

"B-B-Blake, *please,*" Dawn mustered everything she had to speak through the pain. "Whatever you're thinking, I can expla—"

"Did you all *really* take me for an idiot?"

Sebastian stepped forward. "Leave her alo—"

"Felipe, open…the door," Blake commanded as he dragged Beaumont alongside him. Once his loyal employee had done so, he wrenched the petrified veterinarian through to the deck outside of the cockpit.

"Oh my God." Viv had taken Kam's arm, squeezing it as she wished to do something to help. "Is he going to…."

"I don't know," Kam whispered, hopelessness in his voice.

Out in the open, Blake hurled Dawn into the railing. "All in all, you weren't a complete loss, Beaumont." Though the storm had intensified, he didn't take his gaze off of her. "I do appreciate how you kept my assets healthy. It helps when the customer receives a product in good shape."

Dawn only had one last card to play. "But Blake, I thought.... I thought we had something. Wasn't any of it... *real?*"

Sorrow appeared on his face.

Once it faded, he raised the gun. "She's so close now."

BLAM! BLAM!

The impact from the bullets seemed to pin her against the railing.

Before Dawn could even process what had just happened, Blake clutched a fistful of her shirt and thrust his arm forward.

The force pushed her up and over the railing.

From within the boat's cockpit, Viv sucked in a deep breath. *"Noooooo!"*

THIRTY-TWO

"WHERE WERE we?" Blake strolled back inside the protection of the cockpit. "Ah yes, let's put that big blue brolly up now."

Ashbury engaged the diffusion shields while maintaining speed.

From the center of the vessel, an ethereal blueish beam ascended until it reached above the large ship's tallest point. It began spreading out into a canopy, covering the boat's entirety before the front tip submerged into the agitated gale of space-time energy.

"Whoa." Kamren noted how the storm's effects failed to penetrate the barrier. "It's like we're in a bubble."

Motionless, Sebastian had been staring at the spot where Beaumont had been shot and sent overboard. Not only had she been a valuable part of his new SauraCorps community, she'd become a close friend.

One that didn't deserve to die.

Sebastian wanted to call Blake every vile name he could think of. The only thing he could bring to mind was what she'd left behind. "She had a family, you know."

"And she should've thought about them before joining your campaign against me." Back to where he stood in front of the bay of windows, Blake shook his head. "I've kept tabs on all those associated with SauraCorps, past and present. She was a decent fling, I'll give her that."

"You are *the lowest form* of disgusting." Vivienne blurted out what had been on her mind by mistake, but once it came out, she didn't care about his reaction. "I don't even care what miserable story you have to think the world owes you something, or that you can go shooting whoever—"

"*Viv,*" Sebastian called over from across the room, warning in his tone. "Believe me, you don't want to go there."

"Why not?" Blake spun around on his heels to properly address them all. "It's about time we discuss the wonderful gift I'm about to give mankind."

"Go right ahead," Kam remarked with a hint of arrogance. "Villain monologues give the heroes more time to come up with a plan."

A single chuckle slipped out from Blake's mouth. "Really? I'm the villain? From my perspective, that's exactly what *Sebastian* is."

Neither of the teenagers could figure out what to say in reply.

Pacing along the windows, Blake resumed. "Tell me, if you had the chance to harness a law of nature to go back and *save someone you loved,* would you?"

Sebastian piped up. "Time is a law of nature for a reason—"

"And you wouldn't take the chance to go back and fix the mistakes you made with Julia so she'd still be your wife?" Blake whipped back at him. "Have a happy family life?" He gave Sharpe a piercing glare as a crackle of lightning struck the shield close by, which added intensity to his words. "The kind of life I've been robbed of?"

Having lived the same debate years ago, Sebastian stared up at the ceiling in exasperation. "Did you not even see how the rifts nearly tore the world apart a year ago? And now you think you can contain or even control that?"

"With your algorithm, we can."

KA-KA-KA-KA-BRRRRUUUUM!

Viv flinched as the barrage of concentrated whirling density of space-time darkened the room. At this point, she didn't realize how tight she'd been gripping her boyfriend's arm.

"Algorithm?" Kam required more information. "Are you saying there is a way to *control* time travel?"

"Oh, I'm not just saying it." Eagerness flooded through Blake's voice. "Sebastian here has done it."

Part of Sebastian egged him on to waltz over and punch some sense into Arrowsmith. At the same time, another part reminded him of how much Blake had been hurting. "There's more variables to it than you think. We calibrated our pinpoint to the rift energy we had access to." He paused, recalling the experiments they'd conducted. "Only a few mice were sent into the past."

Intent on hearing the outcome, Kam and Viv hung on

his every word.

Pride and regret intertwined in Sebastian's tone. "And… it worked."

"You…." Wide-eyed, Kam rubbed his forehead. "You mean you time traveled without one-point-two-one gigawatts of nuclear power and a DeLorean?"

"The mice did." Sebastian laughed at the movie reference. "Human testing never happened, I shut it down before—"

"Again, you hesitated at the *precipice* of *world-changing* discovery." Blake raised his voice, pulling everyone's gaze to him. "Think of all the things—"

"And that's exactly why I scrapped it!" Sebastian yelled out in frustration, realizing he'd repeated words he'd already said to his former co-worker years ago. "Pulling dinosaurs through rifts is one thing. There were no changes to our present, which means dinosaurs were always meant to die with no affect on our world." His hands balled into fists when he turned back to Blake. "What you're planning, to try and save Claire—"

"Do not say her name as if she is of no consequence!" After those words had exploded from Blake's mouth, the ominous storm crackled and thundered once again. He summoned a shaky breath into his lungs. "It *will* work. I *will* save… my fiancée."

In that moment, Kam's view of the man altered slightly.

As much as Viv sensed Arrowsmith's anguish, she couldn't tear the image of Beaumont getting shot from her mind. "So you *kill* those who get in your way to save your fiancée from getting *killed?*"

Sebastian's eyes flared open more than before. "Viv, careful—"

"Wouldn't you do whatever it takes to save those you love…" Blake wiped away tears that hadn't reached his beard. "…no matter the sacrifice?"

She looked to Kam, who had turned his head to gaze right in her eyes. Her love for him moved her to do many things. A hypothetical situation quickly played out in her mind. "I'd rather sacrifice myself than take someone's life."

Scoffs preceded Blake's reply. "Children are always so naive." To him, the teenagers didn't even matter anymore as he stared back at his old friend. "Give me the algorithm."

Feet planted, Sebastian remained as still as a statue.

The USB with the coveted algorithm sat within his pant pocket.

Like a pendulum, Sebastian's gaze swayed from the innocent kids to the deranged Arrowsmith. If he didn't hand it over, Kamren and Vivienne's lives were at stake. If he surrendered to Blake, their world as they knew it could be altered. *Nothing anyone can say will get him to stop.*

With even more persistence, Blake repeated, *"Give me the algorithm, or they die."*

As for Kam, he'd come so close to proposing. After years of being oblivious to her feelings for him, it didn't take him long to fall for her as much as she did for him. He stood directly in front of Viv to shield her as he looked over at their friend. "Don't do it, Seb."

"Sebastian!" Spit flew from Blake's mouth. "Give me the goddamn—"

176

"S-s-sorry sir, but we're breaking through the storm," Ashbury reported, fairly troubled over witnessing the tense events.

Space-time electricity dissipated.

The thick clouds lessened as they passed by the windows.

Blake hadn't taken his eyes off Sebastian. "Hand it over. There's no escape now that we're past the barrier."

Behind her brave boyfriend, Viv placed her hands on his shoulders as she spotted something not far off through the cockpit's windows. "Oh my God. Kamren, *look.*"

THIRTY-THREE

ABOVE THE ocean, landmass had revealed itself as their destination.

Kamren identified foliage from his time spent on the opposite side of the rift. "Is that a *prehistoric* island?"

Blake never took his aim off the teenagers. "Don't make me ask again, Sharpe."

As Sebastian also gazed over at the inbound island, he fished the USB out of his pocket. He gripped the teeny-yet-vital piece of tech harder than he'd intended to. "Remember, Blake, even one change to our timestream can—"

"*Shut up* and bring it over." Being so close to his endgame, Blake gained even more confidence. "Quit delaying the inevitable."

Slow and steady, Sebastian made his way over. Every step made him increasingly queasy, knowing full well the consequences if Blake succeeded. *I'm about to doom us all.* Only a few feet away from Arrowsmith, he noticed a tall white structure protruding past the trees. Its cylindrical form reminded him of aerospace toys he used to play with as a kid. About to hand the device over, he hesitated. "Please tell me that isn't a satellite."

A swift reach forward allowed Blake to snatch the tiny external drive. "And thanks to this..." He wagged it in the air before pocketing it. "...*Project Pinpoint* will be fully operational. Thank you for doing business." Triumph saturated through his tone. "Take them all away."

Guards seized Sebastian, pulling him back toward the lefthand door.

On the opposite side of the cockpit, Felipe used his gun to direct the kids. "Get going."

Defeat made Sebastian's entire body numb as Blake's men forcefully guided him along. "Vivienne, Kamren...I'm so sor—"

THWACK!

The butt of a guard's gun hammered into the back of his head.

"No!" Viv only saw a moment of Sebastian getting dragged away before she stepped through the other door. Every tense emotion within her burst forth. Dawn had been murdered in front of her. Sebastian had become powerless. The only people left were her and Kamren. *And we're being led to our deaths.*

Kamren slid his warm hand into hers. It reassured and reminded her that no matter what, they still had each other by their side.

She repeated in her mind what she'd said to Arrowsmith

earlier. *I'd rather sacrifice myself than take someone's life.* Every step she took added confirmation to her reasoning. "Kamren?"

With their hands still clasped tight, Kam rubbed his thumb along her skin. "Yeah, Vivienne?"

"You know how much I love you, right?" Her lungs nearly deflated by the end of her question.

Cognizant of the armed man still behind them, Kam nodded as he slowed down. Attempt after attempt, he'd failed to ask her to marry him. "If you only knew what I've been trying to give you this whole time."

Viv turned her head to look at him, but caught the glaring barrel of Felipe's gun within in her peripheral. Back to staring ahead, she whispered, *"Give* me?"

Letting his feet stick to the floor, Kam pulled her back to him. "I can't tell you how incredibly nervous I've been since we started our trip—"

"Keep it *moving.*" Felipe swung his hand up to usher them on.

The teens didn't look at him.

They only kept gazing into each other's eyes.

"Meu Deus, you two understand English?" Felipe gave Kam's shoulder a shove. "Move your feet."

Kam cleared his throat and gave the Brazilian a side-glance. "Do you mind? I'd like to pour out my heart before you shoot it."

Felipe uttered a single chuckle. "One minute."

"We've got a real romantic here." Kam turned his back to focus on the young woman he loved. "Vivienne, we've known each other for almost our entire lives. During those years we spent nearly every day together, and lately…" The intensity of the situation ignited even more passion within his voice. "…I've come to realize that a life without you by my side is a life I never want to live."

"Kamren." Though Viv had been stressed beyond belief, her tone filled with softness. "Are you saying—"

"This isn't the way I wanted to do this, believe me," Kam closed his eyes as he hung his head. "And the ring I wanted to give you is currently inside a freaking dodo bird."

"Phrodo…*ate* a ring?"

"I chased him, made a Lord of the Rings reference you would've been proud of."

Felipe piped up while leaning against the wall. "Ten seconds."

After making a frustrated growl, Kam placed his hands on Viv's cheeks. "Vivienne Lorraine Lancaster, would you do me the honor of being my—"

SKREEEEAAAAOOOOW!

Startled, Felipe lurched away from the wall and readied his weapon.

"The heck was that?" Viv looked away from Kam as soon as the noise occurred.

Kam raised an eyebrow. "We unleashed a lot of dinos, could be any—"

SKREAOW-SKREAOW-SKREAOW!

Four feathered velociraptors turned the corner less than twenty feet away from the humans. They flexed their clawed hands and bobbed their heads to-and-fro while vocalizing.

"Ah, the anatomically-correct velociraptors," Kam noted, placing an arm across Viv to keep them as close to the wall as possible. "Pretty sure Dawn let them—"

BLAM!

SKREEEE-HISSSS!

"Stupid dinosaurs." Felipe swung his gun side to side, constantly having to switch targets as the raptors scurried around.

A limping raptor craned its head to examine its injured leg. Baring its teeth at the Brazilian man, it screeched at its brethren before hissing at the new threat.

"Viv, fetal position!" Kam yanked her to the floor as they tucked into their bodies.

KAOW-KAOW-KAOW!

One of the raptors darted forward, dodged a bullet which lodged into the floor, then launched itself off of the curled-up Kam and onto the armed man. The force of its impact made him stagger back a couple of steps.

With a free hand, Felipe achieved a stranglehold on the pesky velociraptor's feathered neck. "Get off me you little son of a—"

Crunch!

"Aaaaaaaugh!"

Razor-like teeth sunk into his left calf.

As the one raptor gnawed on his leg, another skirted around and leapt onto Felipe's side, knocking the gun away. All three of them weighed him down as they pecked, bit and dug into his flesh with their curved foot talons.

The wounded velociraptor—though slower than the

others—passed the teenagers to close in on the adult human.

Keeping tabs on the creatures, Kam slightly lifted his head. "Normally I'd be miffed by another interruption…" He slowly stood and pulled Viv along to leave the area. "…but this one gives us a getaway."

Before Viv turned the corner, she caught a gruesome glimpse of the attack. "Even with Dawn dead, she managed to save us somehow."

Felipe wrenched an arm back, his fingers mere inches away from the base of his gun. "Help! Someone…help!"

With a final hobbling step, the injured raptor brought its incensed eye right next to the human's.

"Santo Deus…"

Rearing its seething head back, the raptor snarled.

"Por favor—"

Chomp!

THIRTY-FOUR

CRUISING AT an altitude of thirty-three thousand feet, Blake typed an e-mail up on his laptop. His previous deal in Sierra Leone had been successful. He took a moment to lift the lid to one of his forms of payment.

A blood diamond just over five-hundred carat glistened back up at him.

Not too shabby of a tip.

Closing the lid, he returned to the request form for a kronosaurus. He typed in a counter offer to include a couple of saber-tooth tiger kittens at half price.

A facetime call came through on his cellphone, which made him immediately abandon his laptop to pick it up. "Claire, darling, you're out of the appointment already?"

"It doesn't take that long for an ultrasound." His fiancée spoke with an audible smile as she slid into their personal limousine. "And don't even think about trying to weasel the answer out of me."

Blake grinned at her playful nature. "Really? You're going to make me wait until I get home to know what we're having?"

"It's human, I can tell you that much," Claire remarked with a smirk. "When do you think you'll be arriving?"

He noted the time indicated at the top of his phone. "Should be setting down shortly, then I have to take care of something at the SauraCorps UK branch before driving home."

"Will it take you long?"

Blake leaned his head to the side. "It's the first-ever shipment of dire wolves, and if I don't claim some, I'll lose out."

Claire didn't hold back her disappointment. "So you're putting prehistoric *dogs* as a higher priority than your *pregnant fiancée?*"

A grimace showed on his face for a moment. "Once those are in my catalog and sold, my love, our child will never have to worry about a thing as they grow up."

"We already have enough, Blake." She replaced her upset glare with a pleading stare. "Just come home to my... uncomfortably bulbous body and loving arms."

He chuckled through his nose. "I'll be as quick as possible about it all. But as soon as I step through the door, you better have the ultrasound picture in hand."

"Fair enough, Blakey-Wakey." She brought her phone closer to her face and kissed the air. "Love you bunches."

"And I lo—"

Buzzzz. Buzzzz.

Another phone call request came in and partially blocked his view of Claire.

"Oh, this is…. I have to take this call." Blake hovered his finger over the 'end call' button. "Sorry, dear."

Perturbed by the interruption, Claire sighed. "Goodbye, Bla—*oh my God!*"

KEEEERRRRRR-SMASHHHH!

PRESENT DAY

Blake stared at the most recent picture of Claire on his phone. Being so close to the island and his satellite, he couldn't contain his eagerness.

Sebastian had been right.

Every night in his sleep, Blake's dreams terrorized him. Over and over, he'd relive the moment he'd lost the woman he loved and their baby on the way.

I never got to say 'I love you' one last time.

It didn't take much for him to spiral and blame himself for putting business first. The tipping point had come when Sebastian had denied him the use of Project Pinpoint.

Giving the picture one last look, he slid the phone back in his inner suit pocket. Standing front and center of the boat's cockpit, he cleared grief from his throat before addressing his navigator. "Thank you for another successful voyage, Heather."

She nodded. "Yes, sir." Keeping one hand on the computer controls, she reached for her own phone.

"Oh, and before you go contacting your friends at *Interpol....*" Blake turned around and pointed a gun at her. "Bring us in *nice* and *easy* now."

THIRTY-FIVE

"GET THE hatch open!"

An inhale drew salty ocean air into Sebastian's lungs. Coughing it back out, he woke into a groggy state and found himself on the ship's top deck.

Two of Arrowsmith's lackeys held onto him by his arms.

He'd been hauled up to the roof of one of the high-cube container bins.

Grunts came from behind him.

"Throw him in!"

Before Sebastian could even begin to fight back, the men released their grips.

Weightlessness overtook him, sending him downward into darkness.

Thump!

Sebastian landed sideways, his hip making contact with the plywood floor. Though the ten-foot drop didn't cause him to break anything, he winced at the decent amount of throbbing pain. He sputtered, making a plume of dust flow away from his face.

"Grab the chum," someone yelled from above.

As Sebastian's eyes struggled to adjust, he followed the beam of light up to the hatch.

One of Blake's men brought a bucket over to the opening.

"The heck?" Sebastian lurched and rolled away from the falling fish slop. He made it to the metallic wall and huddled up against it. The viscous meat's putrid smell assaulted his nostrils, making him nearly gag.

Then his eyes focused on the mushy pile of fish bits.

Meat.

By now, his eyes had fully adjusted. *Something in here eats…meat?*

The container they'd thrown him into seemed as long and a bit wider than two city buses.

He caught glints of predatorial eyes from the far end.

Hisssssssss!

"Freaking great." He shuffled over into the nearest corner and made himself as small as possible. He hoped whatever it was would focus on the chum instead of making him into a chump. *All those years of searching for carnivores, and one's about to eat me.*

Keeping his gaze just over his knees, he slowed down his breathing.

The creature's head came forward.

It's girthy, cylindrical body slithered along the bin's floor.

As the animal kept closing in foot by unnerving foot, Sebastian couldn't help but reflect on his life. He'd made a mess of his family by focusing on his work at the old SauraCorps. Greed had corrupted his moral compass to the point of throwing people through time rifts to dispose of them. The moment the company had abandoned him to the prehistoric past had changed everything.

Any moment now, he would become a victim of his own criminal past.

A forked tongue flickered out of the creature's mouth, picking up the fishy scent. Turning its head to inspect the slop, it noticed the lack of movement.

Sebastian stiffened every muscle in his body. He couldn't quite identify what kind of prehistoric creature he'd been offered to. Opening his eyelids to slits, he also took a slow, shaky breath.

The tongue flickered out.

Its football-sized eyes scanned around the chum.

Through his eyelashes, Sebastian made out a giant serpent's head. Back in the old SauraCorps days, he'd never come across a full-grown specimen of what he suspected it to be. *Titanoboa. The largest snake ever found, and it's about to find me.*

More oscillating tongue-flicks helped the titanoboa to sample the air molecules.

Letting his chest rise slowly, Sebastian took a silent, deep breath.

The dusty air inside of the large bin hit the back of his throat.

Pulling his Adam's apple inward, he fought to stop his lungs from clearing the irritating blockage.

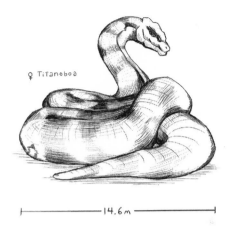

♀ Titanoboa

|———————— 14.6m ————————|

Catching on to a scent, the snake brought its head closer to the corner.

Sebastian's face reddened due to the lack of oxygen.

Thp-thp-thp-thp-thp-thp.

The oversized serpent flicked its tongue, making contact with the sleeve of Sebastian's suit jacket.

Unable to hold onto his breath, Sebastian only had one thought at the forefront of his mind. *Felicia will never know how much I truly loved her.*

Erupting into a coughing fit, he spread out his legs as he let go completely.

Jaws open, the startled titanoboa reared its head back.

Keeping his eyes shut, Sebastian welcomed the oxygen and accepted his fate.

The enormous snake coiled up most of its body and arched some of its front half, positioning its head directly over Sebastian's.

He whimpered and didn't look up.

Thp-thp-thp-thp-thp-thp.

The forked tongue swept against his hair.

Excruciating seconds ticked by.

"Kill me already," Sebastian pleaded, already overcome with numbness. "Make it quick."

Thp-thp-thp-thp-thp-thp.

Again, the top of his head had been tousled by the titanoboa's tongue. None of its fangs pierced into him.

Finally angling his head up to look it in the face, he cried out, "What's the hold up, you big, stupid...."

Mouth closed, the snake's snout drew closer. It brushed against the side of his head before giving him a lick.

Sebastian noticed a golden hue around its eyes. "B-*Bertha?*" Regaining composure, he reached out with a steady hand and ran his fingers along the reptile's chin. "Is that you...girl?"

Bertha turned her head side to side, studying him as if trying to confirm who it had reunited with.

Strength returned to Sebastian's legs as he placed a hand on the wall to stabilize himself as he rose up. "Blake still keeps you as a prisoner rather than a pet, huh?" Avoiding the fish scraps, he raised both hands and gave the underside of Bertha's head more scratches. "You've *definitely grown* since the last time I saw you. Too bad he still relies on others to actually feed and care for you."

Bertha nudged the crook of his neck, which sent its human friend back a step. Ever since Blake had taken her as a spoil from beyond the time rift, she'd received more love and care from Sebastian whenever he'd visited Blake's home.

"Hey, you're a bit big to rest your head there now." Sebastian spoke with a quiet chuckle, figuring he should keep his voice low. He had no idea whether Arrowsmith's men were outside of the heavy-duty metallic container or not.

Enjoying the scratches, Bertha flicked her tongue against the side of his face.

"Snake breath, yum." Sebastian took in the entirety of the makeshift cage. Stopping Blake thrust itself back to centerstage among his thoughts. "Well, if you're not going to eat me, maybe you can help me."

THIRTY-SIX

RACING DOWN a hallway and nearing their room, Kamren slowed down a tad and grabbed at the back of Vivienne's shirt. "So um, now that we haven't come across any twirps, maybe we should talk about what I was about to—"

"Kamren, as much as I'd love to talk about that…" Viv turned her back to their door. "…we need to move it and stop Arrowsmith."

Blindsided by her motivation, Kam pulled his head back. "Uh, you actually think *we* can stop him?"

About to head inside, Viv let go of the doorhandle. "Dawn is *dead*, Kam."

Mention of Beaumont—who'd been helping them all along—made him tuck in his bottom lip.

"And we have *no idea* of what they're going to do to Sebastian," she added, trying to keep herself from becoming frantic. "For all we know, we're the *only ones left.*" After delivering her solemn statement, she entered their room and found Phrodo asleep on the inflatable mattress. "And then there's that to deal with."

"Yeah." He smirked as he walked in. "Should keep the little guy close in case a ring-poop pops out."

"Ew." Viv unzipped a flap to her luggage and pulled out a small hair elastic to form her hair into a ponytail. "Keeping Phrodo in a sweater won't be helpful while trying to save the world, though."

The gravity of the situation agitated Kam's gut. Though he'd been determined to improve on his bravery, his legs betrayed him by locking up. "Honestly, Viv, what do you think the two of us can even do?"

"I don't...." Sighing, she flexed her fingers before rubbing her face. "I don't know, but we need to do *something.*"

Running through the possible variables, Kam shrugged as he raised his arms. "He'll probably have a vehicle and even more guards on the island." Giving it more thought, his face intensified with enthusiasm. "If we use the right motivation, we could possibly use one of the dinos for transportation."

She snorted in retort. "Sorry, you want to try to *ride* something?"

"If Theo could do it with Quinley...."

Vibrations shuddered throughout the entire boat.

A subtle sway in their room gave their legs a balancing test. Creaks and metallic moans indicated the ship's slower and precise movement.

A slight jostle woke the napping Phrodo.

Kam placed a hand to his stomach. "Uh, are we docking?"

"Which means we're running out of time." Viv flung open the flap to her luggage, making sure she'd have everything she needed. Taking the dodo bird into account, she pulled out her compact mirror. "Grab Phrodo."

He squinted at her choice of item. "Gonna check your makeup while we take him down?"

"Birds like mirrors." Clipping it closed, she slipped it into one of her front pant pockets. "If we need Phrodo to move with us, it might come in handy."

"Guess we're doing this then." Kam stretched his arms to make himself more limber. "But if we come across a table with stuff all over it, I'm swiping everything off to pull out a map and go over the plan."

Up on the top deck, a few of Arrowsmith's men stood around Bertha's durable containment box. A couple minutes had passed by since they'd thrown Sebastian inside. While some of them stayed alert to the happenings within the metallic cage, others were relieved by the comfort of land being close by.

Clang! Clang!

Rifle at his side, one of the men turned his attention to the c-bin.

Sebastian yelled through the thick metal door. "Anyone out there?"

The group of guards exchanged suspicious glances.

A guard named Bennett scratched at his scruff and huffed in disbelief. "Give her a couple more minutes. She can't resist the garnish of chum."

"Uh, yeah, about that…." Sebastian paused for dramatic effect. "Either something is really wrong with your snake, or it's *dead.*"

"Impossible." Another guard called back. "She was perfectly fine before getting teleported here."

"And yet I'm still talking to you guys."

Closest to the container, Bennett snapped his fingers at one of his co-workers, then pointed to the top. "Porter, birds eye view." His next orders went to a pair of men standing behind him. "Henderson, Schaefer, unlock the door. Everyone else, weapons ready."

Porter climbed the built-in ladder and made it to the flat top. Once he'd unlocked the hatch, he opened it with one hand while holding his rifle with the other.

As for the other two, they approached the front door with caution in every step.

Henderson disengaged the padlocks while Schaefer grabbed onto one of the handle mechanisms.

The leading tactician called up to Porter, "See anything?"

Bringing his face closer to the opening, Porter shouted back, "Nothing ye—"

Splat!

"—egh." Porter wiped a smattering of slimy gobs from his neck and chin. "What the…. Something just hit me in the face."

Both levers to the main door had been lifted.

"Your face?" Henderson gazed up to see his fellow man still hunched over. "The heck are you talkin—"

"Aaaaaauuuuugh!"

Porter had been yanked inside.

Before everyone else could react, the door flung open with a hard wallop.

An alive and thrashing Bertha exited the bin with Porter's bottom half sticking out of her mouth halfway.

Chunks of fish chum splattered onto the rest of Arrowsmith's crew.

Sebastian rushed behind Bertha and wiped his hands off on the plywood flooring.

Picking up on multiple targets marked with the wafting aroma, Bertha vomited Porter out onto a scrambling Henderson.

She coiled her giant muscular serpentine body, knocking people over in the process, and launched her open mouth at the nearest human.

As the enormous snake's jaws crimped around Bennett, he cried out, "Open...*fire!*"

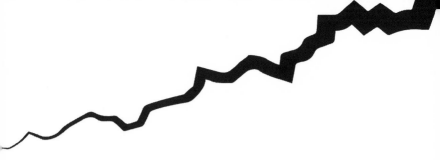

THIRTY-SEVEN

"COAST IS...not clear." Kamren peered through the window to the creature containment room. Even with Phrodo tucked under his arm, they'd managed to avoid detection all the way down. "Looks like they're getting ready to head out."

Most of Arrowsmith's workers had congregated where the teens needed to go.

Vivienne peeked over the bottom of the window and noticed a large hydraulic door lowering down to the wide concrete pier. "See Blake anywhere?"

Taking a closer look, Kam shook his head. "I don't, uh...."

An eager Arrowsmith hustled past the group. "Get a move on, people." Without missing a beat, he marched down the mechanical ramp. "Gorini, get the mammoth calf onto the trailer. We'll use it for Pinpoint's initial test."

Still outside of the room, Kam put the pieces together

with his sci-fi author brain. "Oh my God, I just realized the full capacity of that satellite."

Viv glanced over at him. "Enlighten me, please."

"We're currently on a prehistoric island that's stuck in a spacetime pocket. If he sends that satellite up into this *prehistoric* time…" Kam gestured left and right with one of his hands. "…it could possibly end up in our *present's* atmosphere."

"Because if it existed back then…it would also exist in the now." Mouth open, Viv worked through it with him. "Pinpoint is the *ultimate* time-teleportation device."

"Not only that." Other details bounced around in Kam's head. "Imagine if Blake allowed others to change pivotal points in our history."

Viv brought a hand to her mouth. "Oh jeez. The 'what if' scenarios are endless."

"And horrifying."

Calling out to its mother, Downey the infant mammoth took timid steps behind Gorini.

Other Arrowsmith employees followed the calf, ready to use prods if necessary.

"Poor thing." Viv placed her fingers on the bottom of the window. "Downey is defenseless to them."

THWUMP!

Millie the mother mammoth stomped her foot with hostility.

Already down the ramp and to a jeep's trailer on the pier, Downey received cruel sparking ends of electric sticks. Crying out while unwillingly boarding, he stared back at its mother, hoping she would come to his aid.

Blake hopped into the front passenger seat. "The calf is going to Helsinki, right?"

The driver started up the vehicle. "We'll give them a call to expect it soon."

As the jeep took off, Blake slammed the door shut.

"No, no, he's getting away." Viv reigned in the part of her willing to storm out and summon her inner *Xena: Warrior Princess*. She'd handled a giant millipede, but a troop of armed men seemed a bit dicier. All she could get her hands on: a dodo bird. "If we're going to get past those guys, we need a distraction."

Kam stepped away from the door. "Give me your phone."

"What?" She pulled it out of her pocket. "Why?"

He took it and searched through her downloaded music. "Got any Aerosmith on here? We could blast it from a hidden—"

"Kamren." She slapped his shoulder before swiping it back into her possession. "Can you *please be serious* about this for one—"

BLAM! BLAM! BLAM! BLAM!

Both teens turned their gazes to the window in the door.

The men outside stared upward.

Viv stashed her phone and stiffened. "Were those gunshots?"

"Aaaaaauuuuuugh—"

Crunch!

Someone from the top deck of the boat slammed into the concrete pier.

Kam started to open the door. "Jeez, that's the second time I've heard the Wilhelm scream in person."

Out on the pier, a woman fumbled with her rifle before getting a shot off.

Bertha's massive snake jaws snagged the lady, tossing her around for a couple seconds before letting go. The irate titanoboa slid down to continue attacking Arrowsmith's forces.

Sebastian came down the stairs behind the teenagers. "Thank God you're both still alive."

Viv turned when she heard their older friend's voice. *"Sebastian!"* Energized by his surprise appearance, she greeted him with a relieved hug. "We thought...."

"Nice to see you're not dead," Kam added, filling in for Viv.

A distant yell for help made Sebastian step out into the larger room. "Thanks to Bertha, she's been a big help."

"Big, huh?" Kam held the door open for his girlfriend. "Out of all the words in the dictionary to describe that, you went with 'big'?"

Chasing another guard, Bertha slithered her head past, coiled on a dime, and ended up with a mouthful.

Viv cringed. "Blegh, that's the biggest nope-rope I've ever seen."

"Ah, she's an old friend." Sebastian whipped his gaze all around. "Is Blake already gone?"

THWUMP!

Still wailing for her baby, Millie became even more infuriated.

"They're already on their way to the satellite," Kam reported.

Sympathizing with the giant mammoth, Viv grimaced as she looked up at her. "And they took Downey with them."

Overcome with concern, Sebastian raced over to the opening which led to the pier. "Huh? The actor?"

Finding the question humorous, Kam chuckled. "Yeah, the *Avengers* just recruited a baby mammoth."

Sebastian noticed the rugged and worn road leading off in the direction of the towering white cylinder. He would need to leave immediately to catch up with Arrowsmith. "Listen, I need you both to stay safe here. If anything—"

"Like heck we are," Viv countered, making her way down the ramp. She spotted a left-behind vehicle closer to land. "We can take that jeep over there."

The last one of Arrowsmith's men popped up from the grass and darted for the driver door.

Bertha flicked out her tongue, caught his scent, and weaved toward him.

Getting the door closed, the man had no weapon to defend himself with.

Wrapping her gigantic, smooth body around the jeep multiple times, Bertha constricted her powerful muscles.

Wheels popped and bent.

Glass cracked and shattered.

Metal frame and upholstered interior crimped inward, eventually cutting off the man's shouts for help.

"That's...awesome." Kam lifted his arms in the air and dropped them back to his sides. "Real *big* help she ended up being."

CLANG-THWUMP!

Millie racked her tusks against the cage while still expressing her frustration.

"Dammit." Sebastian raked his fingers through his hair. Though he'd never truly had a plan, he sensed they'd already run out of time. "We're never going to catch up to him now."

"Not with that attitude, we won't." Viv stood by the oversized cage and brought her hand up to the keypad. She silently thanked Dawn once again for showing them the code. "But with *Millie's* attitude, we have a chance."

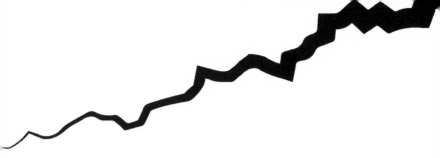

THIRTY-EIGHT

CLAIRE.

She'd claimed the foremost thought in Blake's mind.

Now, by means of Project Pinpoint, his mind wouldn't be the only place.

She'll be in my arms once again.

It amazed him how a complex, potentially world-changing program could fit in the palm of his hand in the form of a USB.

In a few more minutes, it would reunite him with the love of his life.

The driver of the jeep received chatter in his earpiece. "Confirmation just came in. They've uploaded coordinates for the calf's transponder."

Blake fixed his gaze on the looming command center. "Excellent. First, we'll test it by sending it back a minute, still in our facility."

Maintaining the speed he'd been ordered to, Litchfield

gave a skeptical glance. "Sir, I'm, uh…no sci-fi expert, but wouldn't putting the mammoth in the same room with itself break something in the universe?"

Blake gave him an intense glare. "Do I pay you to concoct ridiculous theories?"

After a slight clearing of his throat, Litchfield didn't say a word in response.

Less than thirty seconds of a silent drive later, they pulled up in front of the complex. A small team of scientists and guards exited the facility. Some greeted their boss while others tended to the agitated Downey.

One of the lab techs noticed the USB and stepped closer. "Is that what we've been waiting for?"

Blake grinned, holding up the gadget between his thumb and two fingers. "The information written within this is finally in our grasp. We finally have the key to opening an entirely new method for time travel." He took a moment to take in everyone's excitement, which bolstered him even further. "Everything we've worked tirelessly for, everything we've *sacrificed*…" Exhilaration gave his voice slight tremors. "…has led to *this.*"

When he stopped talking, a different shakiness took form in more than just his voice.

Rumbling vibrated through his feet and up his legs.

A blonde scientist turned left toward the forest. "What… What *is* that?"

Melodic noise mingled with the reverberations.

Another among the group piped up. "Is that… Aerosmith?"

SNAP-CRUNCH!

Trees crackled and parted as underbrush gave way to being trampled.

Millie the mammoth barrelled through.

On top of the prehistoric pachyderm, Vivienne sat closest to its head, with Kam and Sebastian behind her. They'd managed to cling to Millie's thick wool.

Phrodo bounced along sitting in-between the teens.

With one of his hands, Kam held onto Viv's phone, which blasted the main guitar riff of *Sweet Emotion by Aerosmith*. "This…is…*epic!*"

Millie charged forward, bellowing for her young. She angled her tusks down and tossed one of the jeeps aside as if it were a toy car.

"Get the baby to the lab!" a scientist yelled, holding one of the doors open as his colleagues followed their instruction.

Keeping stride, Millie set her gaze on the vehicles and people around the complex's entrance, then zeroed in on her vulnerable calf.

"Inside, now!" Blake ordered, stunned and maddened by the imposing interruption. He scrambled past his employees and whipped one of the glass doors open.

Up on the mammoth's back, Sebastian gripped the long hairs tighter. "Hold on!"

A simple flick from Millie's solid tusks clobbered a Range Rover, sending it rolling.

KER-SMAAAAAASH!

Some dove or stumbled out of the way as the vehicle destroyed the bay of glass doors. The Rover's front end slammed into a technician's back before he could get to safety.

"Should I say it?" Kam climbed down Millie's side, and slid the last couple of feet. "That's one way to make an entrance."

Viv tossed Phrodo to him, then dismounted after. "Or destroy one."

"More on the nose." Kam scratched the dodo on the head. "I like it."

Sebastian had descended Millie from the other side, and immediately ran for Blake's complex. "Come on, we need that USB!"

Getting back to his feet, Blake stared at the decimated section of building and his disarrayed employees. "You've got to be kidding me." Scratching at the back of his head, he stopped mid-itch.

The hand he'd been using once held the USB.

"For God sakes!" Blake swung his gaze around in a frenzy. Everywhere he looked, he only saw shards of glass or rubble. "Where in the bloody—"

"Looking for *this?*"

Blake's shoulders lifted as he slowly turned toward the irritating adolescent voice.

Kamren held the USB between his fingers and stood with confidence. "Guess you can't go on your totally righteous *Excellent Adventure* now, eh, dude?"

Blake's mouth twitched. "Hand it over, *boy.*"

Trotting around the debris, Phrodo came up beside Kam.

Glancing down at the bird, Kam formed a quick plan. "You know, I could…but my bird-bro Phrodo here is a bit *peckish.*" He crouched down and placed the mini storage device in the dodo's bill. "There you go, eat it."

Phrodo didn't open its beak further.

Dooo-dooo.

Kam glanced from the dodo to Arrowsmith and back. "Come on, don't embarrass me."

With innocence in its eyes, Phrodo gawked up at its human friend.

Dooo-dooo-dooo.

Vivienne approached from behind with Sebastian not far off. "Everything okay?"

Kam took his eyes off the Englishman. "Well, apparently Phrodo's fine with eating *a ring*, but when I want it to eat the—"

"Kam, look out!"

BLAM!

A force as if getting punched had struck Kam in the left shoulder before searing pain took over. His arm tensed up, which increased the already incredible amount of agony.

Blake had fired the bullet.

Viv rushed over to her injured boyfriend. "Kam—oh my God—Kamren!"

As Kam crumpled to the tile floor, Sebastian ripped his dress shirt off while rushing over. He placed it on the wound and looked to Viv. "Keep pressure on—"

THWACK!

Blake socked his old colleague in the side of the head.

Blindsided by the strike, Sebastian tumbled back into unconsciousness.

"No!" Viv sprang up to defend herself.

A strong shove from Blake pushed her over and onto broken pieces of glass.

He picked up Phrodo, tucked the bird under his arm, and yanked the USB back into his possession. "Did you all honestly think you could stop me?" Flinging the dodo bird away from him, he clutched the tech even tighter in his hand. "Look at where you all are. This…is…*my…turf.*"

Sucking in a sharp breath through his teeth, Kam kept the shirt on his injured shoulder. "How could we…*aagh*… simply stand by when the world…" Welling up with tears due to the dull throbbing from the bullet, he looked into Viv's eyes. "…and the ones we love are at stake?"

Viv gazed back into his hazel eyes.

She didn't have to say a word.

After all they'd been through, the kidnapping, the emotional tension, nothing could ever stand in the way of their intense love for each other.

"Couldn't have said it better myself," Blake countered, leaving the small group behind as he fled down a hallway.

Keeping an arm around Kam to help him stay upright, Viv struggled to overcome a barrage of negative and hopeless thoughts. "Kam, what are we… I don't… I don't know what to do now, I…." She checked on Sebastian from her position.

Other than breathing, his body showed no signs of liveliness.

"Viv…." Kam winced, trying not to focus on the fact he'd been shot. "Vivienne…you need to stop—*uugghh, frig.*"

Short breaths brought minimal air into Viv's lungs. "By myself?"

She'd experienced many nightmares over the past year.

Now, she found herself living one.

"Kam, I can't—"

"You *can*…." Kam grit his teeth as incessant, unbearable spasms in his shoulder reminded him of his bullet wound. "You found a way before…to push everything asi-i-i-ide… and save E-A when it counted."

Viv commanded her lungs to suck in a needed breath as tears flooded down her face. "That was *way different.*"

"No, it wasn't." Kam placed a hand on her cheek, making her lock eyes with him. "All Blake is, is a disgusting bug… in a suit."

She laid her hand over his and laughed at the imagery. "But I can't just leave you here—"

"Go." Kam rubbed a tear away from the corner of her lips. "Give us a chance for a world where I can marry you."

Viv gave in to her mind imploding with heart-crushing passion. Her mouth collided into his, kissing him in a way which encompassed more than she could ever express with words.

As for Kam, the energy from her lips seemed to momentarily keep the ache within him at bay. Coming out of the embrace, he nodded her on. "You've got this." He lurched up onto his knees. "I'll stay and try to wake Seb up, then we'll make our way to you."

Limping over, Phrodo gazed up at the teens.

Stroking Kam's hair, Viv willed her throat to swallow down a boulder of anxiousness. "If anything happens to me—"

"I love you, too."

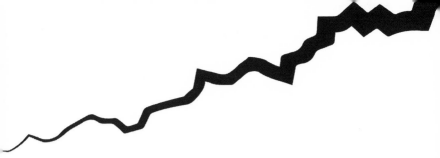

THIRTY-NINE

"ARE WE ready to launch?" Blake marched into the airport hangar-sized control room.

Along the long walls of the area, prehistoric creatures were penned within many cages. Solitary animals paced from end to end of their enclosures. Adult dinosaurs tended to their younglings, upset due to the cramped and confined conditions.

High-tech machinery had been stationed in a corner closest to the door. Multiple scientists and engineers double-checked over diagnostics.

One of the men pushed his glasses back up the sweaty bridge of his nose. "All we need is the Pinpoint algorithm, and we'll be operational."

Impatience festered inside of Blake. "Any chance of launching now and uploading the info wirelessly?"

An engineer piped up. "As long as the connection is strong enough, it should work."

"Do it, Dr. Delton," Blake ordered, handing the USB over to his top technician.

Once Dr. Delton held the gadget in the palm of her hand, every step they took toward the connection port increased their nerves. They were about to be a part of a historic moment in the scientific community.

Inserting the USB, they booted it up.

Delton scratched underneath her ponytail. "Uh…sir?"

"What *now?*" Blake took his eyes off the mammoth calf and made his way over.

A window had popped up on the main monitor.

PASSCODE REQUIRED

"Damn you, Sharpe." Burning red colored Blake's face. "Had a feeling he might've done that. Can we hack it?"

"Might take us a bit."

Tiptoeing down the hallway path she'd seen Blake use, Vivienne slowed down even more as she crept toward a corner. As much as hesitancy wrestled with her courage, she hoped there could be some chance of stopping Arrowsmith.

She peeked around the wall's edge.

Further down, a pair of armed guards had been stationed outside of double doors.

Viv pulled her head back and squeezed her eyes shut. *I can't believe I'm doing this.* Her ribs ached due to the pounding of her racing heart. *How on earth am I going to get past....*

She froze.

Something approached her from behind.

Pit-pat-pit-pat-pit-pat.

Viv recognized the sound of avian feet right away and spun on her heels.

Phrodo waddled up to her with more strength than before.

Doo-dmph!

Viv wrapped a hand around the dodo's beak, restraining its little greeting before whispering, *"Shhhh, be quiet."*

Phrodo responded with a muffled squawk.

Inching her way closer to the corner again, Viv checked to make sure she hadn't been outed by the easygoing bird.

Neither of the guards noticed anything.

Viv picked up the bird and plastered her back against the wall. The essence of time weighed on her mind, reminding her that she didn't have much left to make a move.

Even with its beak closed shut, Phrodo looked up at her and made a brief, quieter call while wiggling its legs back and forth.

Viv squinted at the dodo, glanced past her hiding spot to the open hallway, then back to Phrodo. "Well, Phrodo, this might be your *Mount Doom* moment. Though, Kam would probably say Dooo-Doom."

"Sebastian!"

Ceiling light ambience glowed through Sebastian's eyelids.

Woozy flashes of Blake's fist reminded him of what had happened.

Among the images floating around his mind, Felicia flared up. Some of the last words she'd said to him before he'd been teleported echoed among his recent memories.

"Dude." Kamren nudged his friend with his good hand. "Don't make me wake you with a kiss, man."

Hot blood rushed to Sebastian's head as he laid on the cool tile floor. As he fully came to, he unleashed a deep sigh. "Damn left hook still hurts."

Kam gave him a concerned stare. "He's hit you before?"

Sebastian blinked rapidly. "Grudges are ugly things." Taking Kam's open hand, he pulled himself up to a sitting position. Spots started to fade as he glanced all over. "Viv…." He brought both hands up and rubbed his face. "Where'd Viv go?"

"She's on her way to try and stop the smeghead."

Sebastian wondered if he'd been hit harder than he thought. "Smeghead? What—"

"Red Dwarf reference." Kam shrugged. "Sorry."

Adrenaline pushed Sebastian to stand up. Putting a hand against the wall to steady himself, he had Felicia's words poking around in his bleary head.

"Are you good to go?" Kam groaned, hoping he hadn't lost too much blood. "Not sure how useful I'll be, but Viv will need our help."

Sebastian's vision and thoughts cleared up as he finally stood straight without any aid. After everything he'd been through to get to this point, something poked him in the back of his mind.

Something that could change everything.

"Kamren, I've made a *huge mistake.*"

FORTY

DOOO-DOOO.

The two men standing guard outside of the laboratory made squinting glances at each other. They weren't sure whether the noise had come from within the room they'd been protecting, or somewhere else.

Dooo-dooo-dooo.

One of the guards looked over at his colleague. "Did you say something, Kotzer?"

"I thought maybe that was your phone—"

Dooo-dooo.

Both men picked up on the direction of the noise and turned their heads to the right.

A carefree Phrodo shuffled out into the open.

Kotzer pointed at it. "Isn't that a—"

"Dodo bird, right?" The second guard scratched at his dark stubble. "Must've escaped containment somehow. We should grab it."

Hiding behind the corner, Vivienne heard the distant conversation. As footsteps registered in her ears, she pulled the handheld mirror out of her pocket and waggled it around. *Come on, Phrodo.*

The bird gazed back at her, then resumed watching the approaching armed men.

Viv shook the mirror with even more haste while whispering, "Come *oooon!*"

Dooo-dooo.

"Don't 'dooo-dooo' me!" She heard the steps getting closer and panicked. Frantic, she spied a doorway to a stairwell and booked her way over to it as silent as possible. Keeping the door open a smidge, she continued trying to lure Phrodo over to her.

Seeing flashes of light from the reflective surface, Phrodo's curiosity intensified and fled past the corner.

Kotzer picked up speed, repositioned the sling of his rifle, and stretched his arms out. "No you don't."

Viv closed the door before Arrowsmith's men rounded the corner. Tucking herself low into a hunched position, she hoped to avoid detection.

Phrodo almost made it to the door when a pair of strong hands grasped onto its feathered body. Swinging its legs around, it didn't appreciate being touched by someone unfamiliar.

Dooo-dooo!

"Calm down, little guy." Kotzer readjusted his hold, turning the bird around to face him. "You're heftier than I thou—"

WHACK!

"Aaaagh!" Kotzer dropped the dodo and threw a hand up over his eye. "Damn bird! Patton, get over here."

"Did that *bird* do that to you?" Patton kept a hand on his rifle.

Phrodo flapped its wings while knocking its hard beak against the man's shins.

"Watch out for that hook on the end its beak." With a hand tight against his face, some blood still seeped down Kotzer's face. "Got me square in the frigging eye."

Patton chuckled. "Maimed by dodo, huh?"

Directly behind the stairwell door, Viv noticed one of the men bending over to grab Phrodo. She strained herself to gulp down dread from her throat, then placed her hands on the cool metal door.

In the hallway, Patton cracked his knuckles before putting his hands out. "Never thought a dodo could be a lethal—"

THWAM!

Viv whipped the door open and thrust her knee into the man's head, sending him stumbling to the floor.

Kotzer reached for his rifle with his free hand. "Who the heck are you?"

Acting on sheer instinct, Viv ran at him and grappled onto parts of the weapon. Struggling to lean into the grown man, she realized her strength would ultimately be no match for his. She grunted, still holding onto both ends of the rifle as the guard pushed her away.

Kotzer pulled her back in to try and wrench the firearm away from her. "Get lost, blondie!"

Other than groans and whimpers, Viv didn't say anything. Getting jostled backward once more, she pulled her knee back and closed her eyes to slits.

Irate, Kotzer yanked her forward. "Freaking little—"

Crunch!

His knees buckled.

As Kotzer cried out in absolute agony due to the sensitive area between his legs getting rammed, Viv snatched the rifle off of him, swung her arms back, and hammered the butt end into Kotzer's forehead.

Both men were breathing, but neither of them showed signs of consciousness.

Phrodo still pecked at the first man who had tried to capture it.

Everything spun around Viv as heaviness overtook her chest. In her moment of 'fight-or-flight', she'd never expected to take down two armed guards. *I just...did that.* After running the events through her mind, she stared down at her right hand.

The loaded rifle remained in her grasp.

Blake shot Kamren.

Viv relieved one of them of their keycard, then stepped over and past the unconscious men into the last bit of hallway beyond the corner. Putting the firearm's strap over her shoulder, she glanced down to her left as Phrodo came up beside her and fluffed its feathers out.

She chuckled. "Unlikely team-ups usually get the job done, don't they?"

Dooo-dooo.

"Couldn't agree more." Viv began marching toward the laboratory's double doors. "Let's finish this."

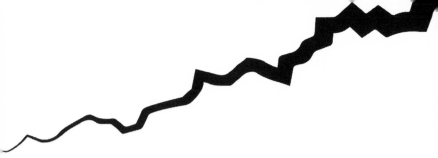

FORTY-ONE

"HERE'S YOUR quantum transponder for returning." Dr. Delton approached her superior and handed over a watch-like gadget. "Make sure nothing happens to it when you're—"

"Yes, yes. Initiate the launch as soon as that code is cracked." Blake attached the transponder to his left wrist, then folded his arms while ordering his staff around. He gazed up to the ceiling where a modified teleportation beacon had been installed.

Blue-tinted shielding encased the circular mechanics. Heavy gauge tubes and wiring spread out from the beacon like spider legs. The tubes filled up with radiating space-time electric energy.

Blake nodded to himself. "Only a few more minutes, my love."

On the opposite side of the door, Vivienne popped her head up to the small window. Taking stock of the employees, she clenched the rifle tighter.

By her side, Phrodo scratched at its neck with one of its feet.

She gave the dodo a small doubtful grin. "Ready for this?"

Dooo-dooo.

"Stay close to me."

Dooo-dooo-dooo.

Viv pressed the keycard up against the reader. After it granted permission with a subtle beep, she slid the barrel end of the weapon through the doorway first. Undetected, she continued entering and let Phrodo in behind her.

Every ounce of blood pulsated throughout her body, producing a buzz she'd never experienced before.

A positive chime rang from one of the main computers. The technician announced, "We're in! Uploading the algorithm now."

Another person in the background responded. "Initiating launch in ten…nine…eight…."

Phrodo cocked its head forward and back, noticing the flashing lights by the command center. Captivated by the blinking buttons, the bird scurried away from Viv's position.

Viv glanced over and froze. *Phrodo don't!*

One scientist spotted the dodo and stopped in his tracks. Following the direction it had come from, he looked straight back at Vivienne. *"Who's the girl?"*

The countdown continued. "Three…two—"

Viv ran out holding up the rifle. *"Stop* the launch!"

Distant rumbling gave the building slight tremors.

A monitor displayed thrusters creating burning clouds.

The crucial cylindrical apparatus headed for the upper atmosphere.

Battling her shaky breaths, Viv realized she'd failed. "Dammit."

"Upload at twenty percent!" one of the technicians reported.

Hearing those words motivated Viv to keep going. "Remove the USB or I'll shoot."

"I'm surprised you can even lift that." Blake remarked, holding his own gun but not pointing it at her. "How'd you get past my guards?"

A corner of Viv's mouth twitched into a smirk. "A dodo bird. Now tell your men to—"

"Thirty percent uploaded," the technician announced.

"Think of this, Vivienne," Blake holstered his weapon back into his pants waistline. "With *Project Pinpoint,* not only can I save my fiancée, *you* could make it so you and your boyfriend never got thrown through a time rift in the first place."

About to reply, she couldn't come up with anything to say. The possibility of going back and manipulating events swished about her mind. She lowered the weapon while pondering how she could avoid the near-death experiences and terrifying dinosaur and human encounters. Her nightmares would be nonexistent.

Changing things would also alter her relationship with Kamren.

After everything they'd been through, they'd reached the

precipice of engagement.

"If we never experience love or the loss of it…" Viv stared Blake right in the eyes. "…then we'd never learn what it truly means to us." Bringing the rifle back into combat position, she aimed at the British man. "Cancel the upload."

"Fifty percent!"

Blake put his hands up in defence. "If I recall correctly, didn't you say you'd rather sacrifice *yourself* than take someone's life?"

Viv fixed her aim on Blake. "Who said I needed to kill someone to stop you?"

She aimed at the command center equipment and placed her finger on the trigger.

"Wait!" Sebastian smacked the barrel upward.

KA-BLAM!

The majority in the room flinched as the bullet rang off the metallic ceiling.

"Seb, what the heck are you doing?" Viv gawked at him in disbelief.

Kamren rushed over to her and glanced up and down from her to the rifle. "Where'd you get…." He opened his eyes wider as he pointed toward the door. "Viv, did you go all *Sarah Connor* on those guards or—"

"I knocked them out." Viv lifted the weapon's strap off of herself. "I didn't kill—"

"Seventy-five percent!"

Blake gave his old friend a peculiar stare. "Had a change of heart, Sharpe?"

"My life is chock full of mistakes." Sebastian ripped the

rifle away from Viv and pointed it at Arrowsmith. "I'm not about to make the biggest one yet."

"Ninety percent!"

Viv yelled out, "Seb, shoot their machines! It'll shut down—"

"No." Keeping his aim on Blake, Sebastian peeked over his shoulder at his young friends. "I…can't."

Bing!

The command center's main screen displayed two simple words.

Blake and some of his crew wore victorious grins as others sighed with relief.

All hope vanished from within Kam and Viv as they stared at the screen. They'd done everything they could, even with the odds against them.

Viv pulled her gaze away from the green letters to the man she thought she'd been helping. "Sebastian…*why?*"

He stared at the concrete floor for a hard five seconds before eyeing up Blake again. "I'm sorry, Viv."

Sebastian didn't need to turn around, because he knew exactly what he would read.

UPLOAD COMPLETE

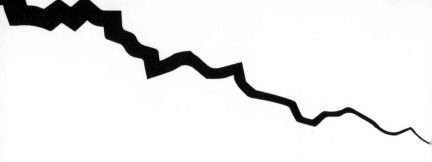

FORTY-TWO

"SATELLITE IS through the thermosphere, linked up and operational," Delton informed with pride and excitement.

"We did it." Blake smiled with a partially open mouth. "Bravo, team! Now let's get the mammoth calf up for our initial test."

"How could you?" Kamren gave Sebastian an unforgiving stare. "We *risked our lives* to stop Arrowsmith, and you just decide to…to throw away the plan?"

Vivienne let her arms slacken. One or two bullets could've wrecked the equipment to keep Arrowsmith from executing his scheme. "Seb, I was *so close* to—"

"There isn't enough room," Sebastian drew out before clenching his teeth back together. "Dinosaurs at my sanctuary keep having babies. Prehistoric life is *thriving* in the present. Soon, there won't be enough room for them."

"So you're…." Kam's mind found a way to connect the

dots. "You want to use *Pinpoint* to send the dinosaurs *back.*"

Sebastian still held the rifle up, following Blake's movements. "Exactly."

Viv rubbed a hand against her face. "But Seb, *you* of all people knew this was dangerous—"

"If it fell into the wrong hands."

Kam looked over at the Englishman standing among the scientists. "Save the dinosaurs, save the world—like the TV show *Heroes*. The satellite was always the key."

Blake stepped forward with vigor. "If you're all done catching up, we have a test to conduct." He neared the time-teleportation transmitter area and eagerly waited for one of his men to lead Downey up to a hexagonal beaming platform.

Glancing around, Kam spoke up. "Viv, wasn't Phrodo with you?"

Realizing she'd lost track of the dodo, she began searching from where she stood. "Uh, it was here a minute ago."

"Let's send our little friend back, oh, five seconds before the exit point. Place its entry ten feet back from the platform." Rubbing one of his palms with the opposite thumb, Blake impatiently waited for his turn. "And when it appears, *do not stop* the countdown! Should avoid any paradoxes with a short window, and we'll see if your algorithm works properly, Sharpe."

Sebastian made little nods. "It'll work."

One of the scientists attached a vitals monitor behind one of Downey's ears, then hooked its leash to a clasp built into the platform. "Subject is secure."

Downey wailed for his mother, failing to yank himself free.

Vibrations in the ground drew Bertha the titanoboa slithering through the forest toward the source. After maiming and destroying humans who had mistreated and prodded her with electric sticks over the years, she had zoned in on a particular scent.

Nearing the compound, she came upon an agitated Millie still stomping her mammoth feet with animosity.

Bertha flicked her tongue out.

The scent she'd been following grew stronger.

She zoned in on the busted entrance doors.

Back in the laboratory, everyone fixed their gaze on the stressed infant mammoth.

A technician raised his voice. "Transporting in five... four..."

Dooo-dooo!

Phrodo scurried out from a hiding spot, attentive to Downey's cries.

The transmitter glowed with blueish, voltaic light.

Viv outstretched her arm and opened her mouth. "Phrodo, no!"

"...one!"

ZEEUU-ZEEUU-ZEEUU-BWOOOOOOOOM!

"Transporting in five—"

ZEEUU-ZEEUU-ZEEUU-BWOOOOOOOOM!

Downey and Phrodo—from the future—appeared ten feet away from the platform, making two of them.

"Holy *Looper,*" Kam blurted out. "It worked."

Dooo-dooo.

The newly arrived Phrodo, upon seeing and hearing its past self, darted around the platform, and intercepted the past bird from getting to Downey.

Dooo-dooo-dooo-dooo!

"…two…one!"

ZEEUU-ZEEUU-ZEEUU-BWOOOOOOOOM!

"Well look at that." Blake hurried over, grabbed some of the woolly hair, and ran his hand along the little mammoth's back. "How's its vitals?"

Dr. Delton approached, checked behind Downey's ear, and monitored the numbers for a couple of seconds. "All looks normal."

"Oh dear Lord." Viv made her way over to the identical dodo birds. "Now there's two Phrodo dodos."

Bzzzzt.

Sebastian picked up on a momentary crackling. He swung his gaze from machine to machine, then lifted his eyes upward.

Glowing energy shuddered around the beacon transmitter.

"Wait, look at…uh, I think that's future-Phrodo," Kam remarked as he tried not to swing his injured arm around. "It's McFly-ing."

Viv squinted at him. *"McFly-ing?"*

Kam crouched and put his hand to it. "See?" For a second, his hand phased through the dodo bird's body. "Because future-Phrodo stopped *this* Phrodo from going back, future-Phrodo is fading from our present timeline."

Viv blinked a few times. "Yup…my brain just imploded."

Fiddling with the transponder on his wrist, Blake positioned himself centerstage on the platform. "Are we ready for me?"

Sebastian pointed up at the beacon's equipment. "Uh, Blake, something's wrong with—"

"Pinpoint is on the co-ordinates," one of the tech's informed. "Just need a timestamp."

Bzzt-fzzt-bzzt.

Sebastian placed a foot on the edge of the metallic stage. "But Blake, look at your—"

"Shut your damn mouth, Sharpe!" Blake's entire face turned red. "All this time, you've been standing in my way, keeping me from trying to *save* her." His whole body heated up as he pulled out and pointed his gun at Sebastian. "And now…" A psychotic laugh burst from between his lips. "…now you think you can keep Pinpoint operational and out of my grasp?"

Attentive to his old friend's trigger finger, Sebastian readied his own. "Playing God with time travel is—"

"Believe me, Sharpe, I've been waiting to play God for

long enough."

Viv snorted. "Dream on, Arrowsmith."

Kam gaped his mouth open. "Oh, so it's okay for you to make song jokes?"

"Enough of this nonsense." Blake took up a ready stance then addressed his science crew. "On my mark."

Sebastian leaned forward. "Goddammit, Blake, you don't know what you're—"

"Three." Cracking his neck, Blake loosened himself up.

Wide-eyed, Kam stared at the determined Englishman. "He's really going to do it."

Glaring down at Sebastian, Blake drew air to the bottom of his lungs. "Two."

Troubled to his core, Sebastian twitched forward. *"Get down* from—"

"One!"

ZEEUU-ZEEUU-ZEEUU-BWOOOOOOOOM!

FORTY-THREE

THWUMP-SMACK!

Sebastian had ditched the rifle and tackled Blake out of the way of the coursing spacetime beam. They landed on the concrete floor beyond the platform and commenced scrapping with each other.

"Bloody idiot!" Blake spat out, still gripping his gun. Pinned down, he leveraged his right arm around Sebastian's extended left arm.

Before the gun could be aimed at his head, Sebastian shifted his left hand to restrain his armed foe. "If you do this…you could *change events—*"

"And Claire would be…*alive!*"

As the two grown men tussled, Kamren observed the crackling column of time-teleportation energy and stepped in front of his girlfriend. "Uh, I don't think it's supposed to be doing that."

Vivienne studied it from top to bottom. "Doesn't it

usually fade after?"

Joining the duo, Dr. Delton lost most of the moisture in her throat. "It's programmed to dissipate once it's transferred the subject."

"Can you shut it down?" Viv took a step backward, frightened of the possible consequences.

"The transmitter, it's fritzing out and flooding itself with energy," a technician yelled out, typing away commands to try and abort the procedure. "We're losing time from when we started. Even if Blake goes through, it may not shut itself down."

Delton attempted to calm herself. "Cut off all power to—"

"Don't you dare!" Blake roared and freed one of his knees. *TWHACK!*

Socked in the gut, Sebastian winced as he tumbled over. *BLAM!*

"*Gaaaaaah!*" Sebastian's gut pain soon became close to nothing compared to the bullet in his right thigh.

Back on his feet, Blake didn't look at his ex-colleague as he headed for the surging spacetime energy.

Though his one arm still hurt, Kam raised his fists. "We can't let him—"

"Kamren." Viv placed a hand on his good shoulder. "I can't... I can't lose you again."

"But you didn't." He lowered his hands and turned to her. "And you never will."

Taking his last few steps to finally saving his fiancée, Blake narrowed his gaze at the transfer point. Everything around him seemed to fade away as his mind and heart shifted into triumphant overdrive. *I'm coming, my lo—*

SMACK!

Blake faltered to one knee. Looking up, he grimaced at the young man who'd struck him on the left side of his face. "Really? You think *you* can take on *me,* boy?"

"Funny." Kam flexed his throbbing fingers before forming a fist again. "Just like *A-ha,* you'll be a one-hit-wonder." He pulled his arm back to make another strike.

The laboratory door broke away from its hinges as Bertha forced herself in.

At the same time, Blake lifted his gun, slipping his finger on the trigger.

Viv screamed out, *"Noooooo!"*

WHA-BAM!

Sebastian body-slammed into Blake, sending them both directly into the effervescing, blueish energy.

FOUR YEARS AGO

"Fair enough, Blakey-Wakey." Riding in the limousine while on the video call, Claire brought her phone closer to her face and kissed the air. "Love you bunches."

Up in his private jet, past-Blake smiled. "And I lo—"

Buzzzz. Buzzzz.

Another phone call request came in his phone. The notification partially blocked the view of his fiancée.

"Oh, this is…. I have to take this call." Blake hovered his finger over the 'end call' button. "Sorry, dear."

Perturbed by the interruption, Claire sighed. "Goodbye, Bla—

ZEEUU-ZEEUU-ZEEUU-BWOOOOOOOOM!

A few feet away from a stretch of sidewalk at an intersection, the clashing men materialized from the future.

When Blake's back struck the asphalt, he accidentally fired off his gun.

The bullet popped one of the limo's rear wheels.

Recalibrating, the limousine driver slammed on the breaks, sending the rear end swerving out of the way of an oncoming transport truck.

"Get *off* me!" Blake shoved Sebastian away and staggered until he stood.

The limo sat only twenty feet away from him.

"Claire."

From within the sleek vehicle, Claire still held her cellphone. "Goodness, that was way too close of a call."

ZEEUU-ZEEUU-ZEEUU-BWOOOOOOOOM!

Bystanders gasped and shrieked in tandem.

More than mindful of his bleeding thigh, Sebastian rolled over to identify the new time traveler. "Oh jeez."

Slithering into the past, Bertha's head narrowly missed the transport truck's front grills.

Cursing at the behemoth of a snake, the truck driver grinded the gearbox and engaged his air brakes. A portion of the giant serpent's body struck the front as the heavy backend of the truck swayed and skidded out of control.

From inside the limousine, Claire recognized the man standing in the intersection. *"Blake?"*

All of time seemed to freeze as Blake zoned in on his fiancée.

Except for the advancing, collapsing transport truck.

Blake screamed, *"Claaaaaaire!"*

KER-SMAAAAAAAAAAAAASH!

Truck trailer collided with the limo. The force slammed the opposite side of the long vehicle into a crosswalk pole.

Other vehicles didn't dare to enter the chaotic intersection as more behind them honked their horns in frustration.

"God, no." With weakened legs, Blake pushed himself on and up to the crumpled limousine. "No…no, no." Only a couple steps away from the crash, he heard a distressed whimper from within. "Claire!" Checking on the driver Mr. Hayes, Blake found him to be unconscious. Making it to the window with edges of broken glass, he carefully popped his head in. "My love, are you all ri—"

"Blake?" Sprawled on the back seat, the lower half of her body had been pinned by the buckled metal and interior materials. The cellphone sat on the floor broken and with a cracked screen. Her right arm sat outstretched toward the window. "You….?" She strained to suck in a hard breath. "You were…on the…plane?"

"I know, Claire, I'm here now." Blake reached in, but could barely touch the tips of their fingers together. "I'm here to *save.…* "

When he looked closer, he lost all breath in his lungs.

Multiple shards of glass stuck out of Claire's left side.

One stuck out from her neck, which had severed an artery.

"I'll get you out, hold on." Ripping off his suit jacket, he folded it and draped it over the bottom of the destroyed window. He grabbed the handle, gripped the covered window edge, and tugged at the door. "Come…on!"

Between the transport's cargo keeping the limo trapped and the crosswalk pole in the way, it barely budged.

"Come *on,* you blasted…. Come *oooon!*" He gazed back at Sebastian, who'd been resting up on the sidewalk. "Sharpe, give me a hand, *please!*"

Cinching his belt around his thigh, Sebastian looked over with solemn resolve. "I'm sorry, Blake."

"You're just going to let her die?" Blake hollered back, then continued to fail at opening the limousine door.

"She already did," Sebastian remarked, saddened to have to relive his old friend's loss along with him.

Giving in to tears, Blake poked his head into the vehicle once more. "Claire, my love, I'm… I'm sorry that I—"

"It's…a boy." Claire managed to say between laboured breaths and managing a smile. "We're going…to have…*a boy.*"

His chin tremored as he entered further. "I know, my love." Realizing she didn't have much time left, he continued. "I'm sorry…that I wasn't here before. I should've never booked a deal at the same time as—"

"Shhhh, it's…all right." She placed a trembling hand on his cheek. "You're here now."

He made it all the way in, took her free hand in his, and kissed her on the forehead before laying his cheek against it.

"I never got to tell you before, I like the name Liam."

"Liam," she whispered with fondness. "I…love…."

Her hand slipped out of his.

Consumed by grief, Blake wept with her head resting against his chest. The woman he'd loved and lost—he'd lost again. Being by her side as she took her last breaths had given him a certain closure among the mourning swirling inside of him.

Police and ambulance sirens sounded off in the distance.

Sebastian approached the limo. "Sorry, Blake, but we have to go."

"Leave me, Sharpe," Blake spat back.

Impatient as the noise grew subtly louder, Sebastian hoped reason would work. "The police will question you, SauraCorps will get involved, and then the world will know there are two of you in this time—"

"If you had *helped* me save her, we wouldn't have to deal with all this."

"I told you it was a bad idea."

Blake gave the top of Claire's head another kiss. "The front of the transport was supposed to hit her. I changed that because… Because you shoved me and messed it up."

Propping himself against the limousine, Sebastian stared down at the asphalt. "Sometimes you can't fix what's broken in the past. All we can do is move o—"

THWACK!

Sent away from the vehicle by a wild punch, Sebastian couldn't grip the crosswalk pole as he stumbled to the sidewalk.

Blake crawled out through the broken window. "You sat there as she *died* in my arms."

"Because she was *always* supposed to—"

WHAM-CRACK!

Sebastian's ribcage took a knee from the raging Englishman.

Snatching close to the collar of Sebastian's shirt, Blake untucked the gun out from the back of his waistline. "It could've worked if you hadn't meddled."

Unable to maneuver himself into a better angle, Sebastian seized each of Blake's wrists. "You abducted me...for the algorithm."

Blake leaned in close. "And now, I'm going to kill—"

Hisssssssssssss!

Bertha burst forward, knocking Blake away and closer to the limo. Partially injured by the transport truck, she limp-slithered toward her cold-hearted owner.

Recognizing the creature, Blake aimed right at her. "Bertha, you bloody stupid snake!"

BLAM! BLAM!

The first two bullets hit Bertha, but as she weaved and darted back and forth, she dodged most of his other attempts as he unloaded everything he had.

Recoiling, Bertha drew the majority of her scaly body in close to her, overlapping girthy sections. She catalogued all the pain points throughout her bulk, then refocused on the human source.

Blake pointed the gun at her again.

Click.

Nothing exited the chamber.

Click. Click.

"Dammit." Blake didn't have another magazine of bullets.

Attentive to the lack of resistance, Bertha hissed while gliding forward.

Terror poured through Blake as he whipped the empty weapon at her, only to have her jerk her head back to avoid it. He dropped to his knees, completely overwhelmed by his loss and failure.

The titanoboa opened her massive jaws wide.

"Bertha, *stop!*" Sebastian hobbled in front of Blake and held both hands up in defence. "Leave him alone."

Curiosity flashed through Bertha's eyes as she gave him some side-eye.

Behind Sebastian, a dumbfounded Blake stared up at him. "Wha...what? *Why* would you—"

"Because I know what you've suffered." Sebastian glanced over at the demolished limousine. "And suffering doesn't deserve death."

Like a hand moving debris through water, Bertha reached out with the tip of her tail and nudged Sebastian off to the side.

Sebastian tried to fight against it and ducked under the tail. "Blake, no!"

Bertha's mouth came down on the cowering Blake, capturing him by his side leaving his left arm exposed.

As agony seared through Sebastian's thigh, he leapt for the arm and snagged the wrist. "Let...him...go!"

A strong flick of Bertha's head shook Sebastian off.

The time-teleportation transponder unclipped into his hands as he fell back to the asphalt. By the time he gazed back up, he caught the last glimpse of Blake's shoes descending past Bertha's jaws.

Sebastian hung his head, then picked it back up as police sirens closed in on the scene.

FORTY-FOUR

PRESENT DAY

KAMREN PULLED his arm back to punch Blake again.

The laboratory door broke away from its hinges as Bertha forced herself in.

At the same time, Blake placed his finger on the trigger while lifting the gun.

Vivienne screamed out, *"Noooooo!"*

WHA-BAM!

Sebastian body-slammed into Blake, sending them both directly into the effervescing, blueish energy.

ZEEUU-ZEEUU-ZEEUU-BWOOOOOOOOM!

They vanished from the present timeline.

Though the scientists had been thrown into a frightened tizzy, Bertha ignored their shrieks and yells as she kept following Arrowsmith's scent.

Viv backed up into Kam. "Whoa, she's going for the—"

Z E E U U - Z E E U U - Z E E U U - Z E E U U -
BWOOOOOOOOOOM!

Head to tail, Bertha slithered into the past.

"Cut the power, now," Dr. Delton instructed her team.

It took two men to heave on and disconnect the high-tech transmitter's cords from the main power. Once the electrical prongs left the generator, only a few sparks formed before the equipment died down.

A haphazard chorus of deep breaths flowed through the lab.

"That snake's about to go where no snake has gone before." Kam draped an arm over his fiancée's shoulders and pulled her in close. "You good?"

"Uh, yeah, I'm...." Viv shifted herself in to him. "I should be asking you, though. How's your arm?"

"It's just a flesh wound." His usual smirky expression quickly turned into a wince before staring over at the Pinpoint platform. "Wonder how long it'll take for—"

ZEEUU-ZEEUU-ZEEUU-BWOOOOOOOOM!

Though the indoor teleportation system had been taken offline, the Pinpoint satellite worked perfectly from its position in space.

Saddled upon a portion of Bertha's bulky body, Sebastian glanced around before zoning in on the teenagers.

"Sebastian!" Viv rushed over, thankful to have another familiar face around. "I...don't even know what to ask you. Are you okay?"

Dismounting the titanoboa, he faltered as his wounded thigh gave him a painful reminder. "I've been better."

Kam studied the furrowed brow and despondent expression on their older friend's face. "I take it things didn't go slitheringly back then."

Halting mid-step, Sebastian placed both feet on the floor. He'd expected the events of Claire's demise to affect Blake somehow. Even with the alterations to how things played out in the past timeline, Sebastian never thought he'd be as moved as he'd become.

Arrowsmith had allowed his grief to turn him into a monster.

In the end, it had consumed him whole.

Stepping forward, Dr. Delton inquired, "Where's Blake?"

Pity weighed Sebastian's face downward, but he managed to look back and lift an eyebrow toward Blake's location.

It took Viv a moment before she glared and pointed at the oversized snake. "He's...*inside* of Bertha?"

About to make a snarky comment about indigestion, Kam took Sebastian's countenance into consideration and said nothing.

Taking a few seconds to gather his thoughts, Sebastian made eye contact with most of the group of scientists and technicians throughout the laboratory. "As of this very moment, I'm offering to employ each and every one of you. What we have access to..." he raised his hand, directing their attention to the spacetime transmitter. "...is a means of resetting the wrongs SauraCorps—and many others— have committed." A spasm in his leg caused him to buckle, but Viv came to his aid by getting under his right arm. "We can work to protect prehistoric creatures from ending up in the wrong hands and then relocate them to their own time. If you accept, I'll be grateful to work along with you. If not, then there's…." His glance to the broken door turned into a double-take as he grimaced. "Uh, you're free to go."

Within the duration of ten seconds, none of Arrowsmith's former team budged.

Sebastian grinned, pleasantly surprised and impressed by their choices. "We have a lot of work to do."

FORTY-FIVE

FIVE MONTHS LATER

JAMMING OUT to *Life Was Easier When I Only Cared About Me by Bad Suns* in his pickup truck, Kamren reversed into the driveway of his family home. He hopped out and made his way up the front walk.

The front door opened, and his mom Cassie brought out a full cardboard box in her arms. "There's only a few boxes left. We may have opened up a couple again just to reminisce a bit."

"Mom, I'm moving out, not dying." Kam poked her in the side while passing by. "And we'll have you over more than once, I promise."

"It better be more than *once*," she countered, balancing the box on her thigh as she lowered the tailgate. "Or else we'll be dropping by when you least expect it."

Keeping the door open as he stopped in the doorway, he

chuckled. "I'd be careful about that, Mom. Viv and I will be doing what *newlyweds* do by then."

"Oh, you mean playing videogames?" Evan Eckhardt piped up as he approached his son from inside of the house. "And sharing cat videos on your phones while sitting right beside each other?"

"Uh huh." Kam smirked as he received another moving box from his father. "Games and cat videos, yup."

"I'll admit, it's going to be different not having you around," Evan remarked with a tightness his voice. Picking up more of Kam's belongings close to the door, he cleared his throat a tad. "I um... I know I don't say this enough, Son, but I'm very proud of the man you've become. You've been through so much in the last while, and I can't tell you how much you've impressed me with how you've handled it all."

As Kam walked side by side with him to the truck, he wore a sheepish smile. "Thanks, Pops. But are you trying to get me all emotional before my wedding day?"

"Oh, I've already rented my poncho dress suit." Evan set his box down on the truck's bed and patted his son on the back. "I know you won't keep it together as soon as you see her walk down that aisle."

Cassie came up beside her boy and snickered. "And I've already got my bets in that you'll be crying the most that day."

Kam laughed at them until his cellphone buzzed in his pant pocket. "Saved by the fiancée." He stepped away from his parents and accepted the call. "Future husband here, how may I be of assist—"

"They canceled the venue, Kam!" The dismay in Vivienne's voice had been more than noticeable. "Apparently a *stupid* water pipe burst and of course, the only time they can get *stupid* renovations done is around our *freaking* wedding date next week."

Kam had pulled the phone away from his ear the louder she got, then placed it back to reply. "Okay, well…did they offer to rebook later?"

"They're slammed until *stupid* spring of next year."

Scratching the back of his head, Kam released a sigh of disappointment. "Too bad we can't just time travel to…. Hey, wait a sec."

After a silent moment of suspicion, Viv responded, "What? Kamren, what are you thinking?"

Kam nibbled on his bottom lip as he formulated a possible idea. "I'll call you back asap. Love you, future wifey!" After hanging up on her, he opened his contacts and scrolled. He tapped on the person he wanted and swiped right to call them.

"Hey, Kam," Sebastian answered, trying to talk over noises in the background. "Kind of in the middle of—Uh, Driscoll! I need you in New York for some pachycephalosauruses. Yeah, something about a café—*hey, buddy, hey!* Watch the ankylosaurus's tail, that'll break all of you with one swing. Make sure everyone clears the platform for transport."

"Sorry, Seb, I just wanted to ask one thing."

"What's up?"

Kam took up a confident stance as he continued. "Remember how you tossed Viv and I through a time rift, and then by helping you out we inadvertently got caught by the kingpin of all dino dealers and thought we were going to die on his boat?"

Sebastian grunted along with an audible eye-roll. "Vaguely."

"Yeah, well, we lost our wedding venue, and I was thinking you could help us to have it somewhere *epic* instead."

"Epic, huh?" Sebastian replied with a hint of curiosity. "What did you have in mind?"

FORTY-SIX

STANDING BY a rustic wooden trellis in a fancy navy-blue suit, Kam flexed his hands open and closed over and over again.

The wedding day had finally arrived.

Outdoors in an open area with perfectly green grass, the stage sat at the end of a few rows of chairs. The quaint amount of family and friends waited for the bride to arrive.

Viv's little brother Arty stood beside the anxious groom in a similar outfit. "Gotta relax, bro. This day is already amazing, and everything else will be, too."

"I know." Kam exhaled a long breath. "I mean…I've faced life and death experiences, and somehow this is making me more nervous."

"Listen, Kam, if there was a word for more than perfect, that's what you and my sister are for each other." Arty spoke from the heart, though still in his youth. "And I'm not one to get into all that mushy stuff."

A small laugh came out of Kam. "Thanks, future-bro. And you've got the ring all cleaned up and ready, right?"

"Yeah, I—wait, *cleaned* up?" Arty placed his hand on the pocket where he'd stashed the ring. "Why cleaned?"

Kam placed a hand on the boy's shoulder. "Because it used to be inside of Phrodo."

Dooo-dooo-dooo.

They looked over at the dodo bird standing just a few feet away. A custom black bowtie hung on its neck, which Phrodo scratched at with one of its feet.

Arty stuck his tongue out and pretended to heave. "Gross."

"I'm kidding," Kam chuckled. "We had it cleaned immediately after he pooped it out."

Felicia Voorhees sat close to the front left of the seating area in a purple dress. Holding a high-tech walkie-talkie style phone with glowing electrical blue indent lines, she gazed around at the serene setting.

Coming over, Kam sat a couple chairs away from her. "Felicia, hey, thanks for helping us set all of this up."

She raised both of her eyebrows in an unsure fashion. "Let's just hope all of your close family and friends here take their NDAs seriously. And remember, we can't let everyone stay late, or else this place will get a little more—"

Kssshhhh-ksshh-ksshh.

The glowing phone crackled to life.

"Hey, Fi, you there?" Sebastian's voice came through.

Placing the walkie closer to her mouth, she nodded. "Yep, is it that time?"

"Tee minus thirty seconds-ish."

Taking the cue, Kam left to go back to the stage. "Talk later." As he walked backward down the middle aisle for a few steps, he cupped his hands around his mouth. "All right, everyone, the bride will arrive very soon, so if you could all take your seats."

The intimate mix of people bustled back to their chairs.

"Better get back there, Arty," Kam instructed the kid. "Or else the bridesmaid will be walking by her lonesome."

"On it." Arty began a quick stroll to the back.

Distant cries made Kam look around at the surroundings. They didn't bother him at all, because nothing could ruin his day. *I'm about to get married.* He took a slow and shaky breath. *I'm about to marry Viv—*

"Deep breaths, my friend," a mature voice instructed from behind him.

Kam turned and shook a familiar redhead scientist's hand. "Thanks, Theo. Make sure you get some money shots, okay?"

"Oh, you betcha." The bearded Dr. Lewis brought a camera to his face and snapped a picture of the eager groom. "You look dashing."

"Why thank you, kind sir."

Positioned behind a makeshift decorated wall, Arty waited for the rest of the wedding party to arrive. A boyish grin appeared on his face as he spotted a massive pterosaur as tall as a giraffe drinking from a pond. "Wonder what it would be like to ride one of—"

ZEEUU-ZEEUU-ZEEUU-BWOOOOOOOOM!

Adorned in a white dress, Vivienne appeared a couple of feet away from her brother. "Man, what a trip. Never thought I'd see this place again, but the circumstances are much *safer* this time around."

Once the awe of the time-teleportation beam faded, Arty whistled at his sister. "Yeah, Kam's gonna bawl like a waterfall."

Viv snorted. "At least he doesn't have makeup to worry about."

He gave his sister a big hug. "And hey, you actually don't look half bad, Sis."

She gave him a light punch. "That suit kinda helps your face, too—"

"Better get *moving*, guys," Emily-Ann butted in with a low voice. "The music just started."

Arty held out an arm to E-A, and they exited from behind the wall and began strolling down the walkway.

The music made E-A squint for a moment, and she whispered, "Is that...a piano rendition of the *Jurassic Park* theme song?"

Arty giggled. "Isn't it epic?"

As they ended their walk, they took their positions in front of the stage.

Kam grinned as he nodded, then mouthed to the sister he'd adopted, *I've missed you.*

Catch up later, E-A mouthed back, then leaned her head to point down the aisle.

Viv stepped out from behind the partition.

Half a second later, Kam couldn't contain his tears.

Andrew Lancaster wore an emotional and proud smile as he walked his daughter down the aisle. His expression changed to a gaping mouth.

Far beyond the trellis setup, a herd of long-necked apatosauruses strode along the top of a low hill. Their bellows intermingled with the dinosaur-themed wedding march, giving everyone attending a surreal moment of glee and astonishment.

"Keep walking, Dad." Viv gave him a little pull, and he obliged.

"This is…" It took Andrew a second to find his breath. "…amazing."

Arriving at the stage, Viv received a kiss on the cheek from her father, then stood beside the man she'd loved for so long.

Kam shook hands with his soon-to-be father-in-law, then locked eyes with his stunning bride, and whispered, "Vivienne, you look… There's *no words.*"

She raised her shoulders as she grinned. "You look quite handsome. And I can't believe we're doing this *here.*"

"What can I say?" He smirked. "We needed a wedding of *prehistoric proportions.*"

Sebastian made his way up on stage, and took his place behind the podium. "Welcome, everyone. Today we're gathered to celebrate and witness the marriage of Kamren Eckhardt, and Vivienne Lancaster…."

END CREDITS SCENE

"I'VE GOT a pair of dryosaurus, half a dozen gastonia infants, and one majungasaurus on the docket for tomorrow so far." Sebastian reported over his spacetime-integrated phone. Late in the evening, the light from his laptop had been his only light source.

"Sounds good, Seb." Emily-Ann Lewis responded from the prehistoric past. "Hear that dad? We have some young gastonias on the way."

Theo stood a few feet away and snapped a picture of an archaeopteryx family up in a tree. "Really? Maybe we can introduce them to the heard we found."

Sebastian could hear the distant voice of the scientist, then spoke to E-A. "Your father's still loving it out there, eh?"

E-A laughed. "He's in his glory. And honestly, I feel like I finally have a refreshing and rewarding purpose in life."

Smiling at her candid words, Sebastian nodded. "And thank you again for helping me out with relocating these creatures to their proper time." His stomach growled, reminding him that he'd skipped dinner to keep working. "Oh, and if you ever want me to send back a pizza or anyth—"

ZZEU-BWOM!

Ominous blueish-white light lit up a corner of Sebastian's office for a second.

E-A groaned as her tastebuds recalled delicious flavours. "Pizza sounds grea—"

Hanging up, Sebastian sprang up and off his chair.

An outline of a person stood in the room's corner.

Backing up toward the light switch, Sebastian pointed. "Who... Who are y—"

"You're Sebastian Sharpe, correct?"

Sebastian placed his hand over the switch beside the office door. "Who's asking?"

Click.

The light in the middle of the ceiling turned on.

A man in a black tactical suit and blond hair remained where he'd arrived. "Do you have any idea of the kind of power you're in control of?"

"I have an idea, yeah." Absolutely dumbfounded, it occurred to Sebastian that the man had teleported into his home by an unfamiliar source. "Wait, did you use my satellite?"

"Not exactly." The mystery man slipped off his high-tech goggles as he stepped forward. "My name is Brett Gallagher. I need your help returning someone to their home planet."

An overwhelming buzzing struck Sebastian's comprehension. "Did you just say...*planet?*"

You better not have time traveled to the
end of this book and read the ending first,
(I'm looking at you, Dad)
but if you enjoyed this book,
please take a moment to

GIVE IT A REVIEW!

MORE FROM DEREK BORNE

THE ULTIMATE AGENT SERIES

The Ultimate Agent – Book 1
The Helios Files – UA Classified Anthology
The Ultimate Agent – Book 2
The Ultimate Agent – Book 3

DINO-RIFT

SIDE NOTE:

There are subtle ties to the Ultimate Agent universe
within *Dino-Rift* and *SauraCorps: Salvation*.

ACKNOWLEDGEMENTS

AS PER usual, the first acknowledgements always go to my wife. This book might as well also have your name attached to the front cover. For the number of times you've sat there as I stared at you trying to come up with a word, you still accept me as your husband, and I'm more than grateful.

To my lovely editor, R. A. Milhoan, is it possible to keep having so much fun working on a book together? I submit, yes. You're such an integral part of the process because you're not just my editor, you're an awesome friend!

To my cover artist, Molly Phipps at We Got You Covered, even though this sequel wasn't supposed to exist in the first place...you made it so these two books in the series look FAN-FREAKING-TASTIC with a side of EPICALLY AWESOMENESS side by side...I want to cry because they're so gorgeous!

To my Betas Lisa, Amanda, Cassie, Jo, Lisa, Stacy, and newcomers Julia, Jenaiya, and Shannon, you're an incredible team that knows how to tell it like it is, and each and every one of you keep helping me to shape these books into the best versions of themselves.

To my fellow authors and readers, my bookish family, and those that screamed for more in the Dino-Rift world... THANK YOU for pushing me to do this, because this book was a BLAST from the past to write!

Be someone's hero, don't take time for granted, and keep moving forward.

DEREK

FAN ART BY JULIA STEPHENS

ABOUT DEREK BORNE

DEREK BORNE is a Canadian author who lives in "the prettiest town in Ontario" with his wife and moody bearded dragon, Ziggy. Always telling stories since a young age, he first wrote The Ultimate Agent at fourteen, and kept writing as a hobby over the years until finally publishing. When he isn't writing, he's selling olive oil and balsamics, watching hockey, and waiting for the next superhero movie to come out.

Find out more at **derekborne.weebly.com**.